Salute!

Linda Shinder

Contents

1	1
2	11
3	20
4	29
5	37
6	43
7	49
8	56
9	63
10	70
11	81
12	92
13	102
14	112
15	121

16   129

17   139

18   151

19   162

20   172

1

A delaide Kaine as Lily

"I'm sorry sir. If you don't take her in, then she will be sent to live with a foster family."

"Are you sure there are no other options?"

"Yes, I have already checked. You are the only living relative."

With a great sigh, General McKain stood up from his desk which was strewn with various documents. His chair scraped lightly against the hard wood floor. He walked over and stood looking out of the window. His gaze fell on the dorms that at this point were empty, but soon would be full.

"Okay." He reluctantly agreed.

He turned to face the man that had brought this predicament to him. Upon entering, he had introduced himself as Mr. Gerston. He was a rather short and plump man with a heavily receding hairline. Compared to himself, he looked as if he could be a midget. General McKain was a tall man standing at 6'6. He had deep brown hair that was peppered throughout with gray.

"I'm glad that you could do this. It is so much better for the girl." Mr. Gerston stated as he rose from his chair and went to shake General McKain's hand.

Without any more words being exchanged General McKain shook Mr. Gerston's hand and watched him as he left. After the man had left, he returned to his seat behind his desk, his head buried in his hands. He had never expected this. Never. He was not ready for this.

"Lily, Lily! Come downstairs!"

"I'm coming!" I yelled as I jogged downstairs to meet my mother who had been yelling for me.

"Your Dad and I are going out for dinner. You wanna come?" She asked.

"Nah. You two go. I'm not that hungry, " I replied.

"Okay. I'll have my cell on if you need anything, " my mom reminded me.

"I know."

My mom smiled at me. We went though this routine every time she left the house. You could say she was a little protective and worried easily. My dad on the other hand was a lot more laid back and easy going.

"Bye, Lily. Be good, you know all that junk." My dad said as he kissed the top of my head and left arm in arm with my mom.

"Yeah, yeah. Have a good time." I called to them as they got into their car and drove away.

'Hm…. What to do?' I thought to myself.

Well after maybe a grand total of two seconds, I ran upstairs to my room. I grabbed the remote to my stereo and turned the volume up to the max. I immediately grabbed my brush, ahem, microphone. I love turning my stereo all the way up. My parents always complain about how loud it is then make me turn it down, but they were gone so it was gonna be loud. I loved the way it made the walls tremble and the floors shake.

About an hour later, I had completely tired myself out. You know pretending to be a rock diva is very tiring. I twitched my stereo off as I trotted downstairs and into the kitchen. The minute I opened the refrigerator, the doorbell rang.

'I don't want to buy any stupid subscriptions!' I thought as I opened the door.

How I wish it had been a salesperson. Standing in front of me were two cops. One was a man that looked to be in his early forties, and a woman that seemed to be in her mid thirties.

"Are you Lily Daniels?" The man asked me.

"Y..Yes." I quietly stammered out.

"I'm very sorry. Your parents were involved in a fatal car accident," he said.

It felt as if the wind has just been knocked out of me. My knees gave out as I sank to the floor in shock, my hand still clutching the handle.

"They were hit, head on by a drunk driver on the wrong side of the road--"

That was all I heard. That was all I needed to hear. My parents were dead. Gone from my life forever! That couldn't be possible! Only an hour ago I had been standing right here talking to them! My chest felt heavy and it was getting hard to breathe. My cheeks were stained with tears that I didn't know I had been crying.

The next three days all seemed like one big blur to me. The funeral, the burial, all of those people hugging me and telling me how sorry they were. However, one thing stuck clear in my mind. I was in a small stuffy office with a short and plump man with a receding hairline. He introduced himself as Mr. Gerston. He was my parents' lawyer. We had been going over the will and I wasn't really paying attention. That was until he got to the part of what would happen to me.

"It is the wish of Trevor and Kathy Daniels that their daughter, Lily Daniels, be put in the care of Eric McKain, their only living relative." He finished reading from my parents' will.

"So what does that mean?" I asked him confused.

"It means that you will be going to live with your uncle... in London."

"London, Kentucky." I was okay with that, it wasn't too far from where I lived.

"No. London, England." He stated simply as if moving to a new country was no big deal.

I sat there in shock. I had lived in Kentucky my whole life! I had never even visited another country, let alone move to one! Not to forget that I hadn't seen my uncle since I was nine, and considering that I'm now sixteen, that's oh about... SEVEN YEARS, and now I have to live with him.

Well now that I've gotten you all caught up, we shall return to the present.

It had been a week since I was told that I would be moving to London, and here I was sitting in a faded orange plastic chair, waiting for my flight number to be called. Glancing down I saw my pink flip-flops and my two small carry on bags.

"Flight number 149 to London, England is now boarding." The female voice buzzed over the intercom.

Sighing, I hoisted my bags from the ground, after pulling down my light pink, and white striped polo. I slowly made my way to the terminal.

"This is it. My whole life is going to change," I told myself.

Once I had placed my bags into the overhead compartment, I flopped down into my seat and pulled out my Ipod, along with my newest issue of Seventeen. Turning the volume up on my Ipod to drown out the world around me, a small smile crept across my lips. 'Miss Independent' by Kelly Clarkson came blasting through the earpieces. I had always loved this song.

About half way through my flight, I woke up with my magazine still opened in my lap and 'Move Along' by the All American Rejects blasting into my head. I turned off my Ipod and got up to use the bathroom.

Stepping into the small, cramped bathroom, I locked the door, and turned on the water. I splashed water onto my face and rubbed the sleep out of my almond shaped brown eyes. I ran my fingers through my shoulder length dark brown hair getting out the tangles. I brought my head up to look into the mirror. GOD! I looked horrible. There were dark circles under my eyes, and I looked pale.

'I can't spend the rest of my life like this! I can't keep feeling sorry for myself! I don't want this to ruin my life. I've mourned, and now I'm ready to move on. I'm gonna make the best of my life!'

After my little metal self pep talk, I walked back to my seat.

The rest of the flight had rather boring. Consisting of an overly happy flight attendant that kept asking me if I wanted some peanuts, a total of four times, and a three year old boy throwing a tantrum because his mom wouldn't let him have the peanuts. I thought I was gonna go crazy! Thankfully the pilot's voice came over the speakers.

"Ladies and Gentlemen, we will be landing in London, England shortly. Please fasten your seat belts and remain seated until further notice. Thank you for flying with American Airlines, have a nice day!"

'Finally! If that lady offered me one more bag of peanuts, I was gonna shove them down her throat!'

That same flight attendant brought me out of my thoughts.

"Miss we have landed. You may now undo your seat belt and exit the plane, " she said, smiling the whole time.

Mumbling a quick thanks, I undid my seat belt and got my bags down from their prior-resting place. Walking out into the aisle, bags in hand, I waited as the other people slowly shuffled off the plane. I ended up waiting behind the mom with the three-year-old boy, who was now peacefully asleep in her arms with his thumb in his mouth.

After waiting for ten minutes, I finally stepped off the plane and into the airport. I grabbed the rest of my luggage from the waiting station and proceed towards the exit to find the find that I had been told would be waiting to pick me up.

After a while of waiting, I spotted a man dressed in army attire holding a small white sign with clean black letters that said DANIELS.

"Hi." I said as I approached him.

At first he looked a little confused but shook the look from his face and replied with a stiff 'hello'. He grabbed my luggage and put into the trunk of a black car. He then opened the back door and waited for me to get in.

"Thanks." I offered with a small smile as I climbed in, he shut the door behind me without responding.

The car ride was long, silent, and uncomfortable. He kept glancing at me in through the mirror, with a weird look in his eyes. It looked like curiosity.

After forty-five silent minutes, I found myself looking out the window to see a sign that read, 'Wilmington Military Academy for – ' I didn't even finish reading the sign, I was shocked.

'That just said Military Academy! I'm supposed to go live with my uncle, not go to Military school!'

"Miss, we're here." The man stated from the front seat.

He got out of the car and opened my door. I slowly climbed out and said a quiet 'thank you.' He nodded his head and went to get my luggage out of the trunk. I looked around in amazement taking in the surroundings.

There were four identical buildings each made out of deep red brick and three stories high. Off to the side were several smaller buildings that looked like offices. On the opposite side sat a large three-story building, which seemed to resemble a school. Off in the distance I caught a glimpse of what looked like an obstacle course.

'OKAY! I AM NOT DOING AN OBSTACLE COURSE!' I screamed inside my head.

"This way miss." The man said as he headed towards one of the buildings that looked like an office carrying your luggage.

I followed behind him carrying the two small bags I had taken on the plane with me. We reached a small red brick building. I waited as he knocked on the oak door.

"Come in!" Came a deep voice from behind the door.

He opened the door to reveal a small office with a man in his mid to late forties that had dark brown hair that was peppered with gray, sitting behind a large mahogany desk. The man that had brought me here nodded his head in the other man's direction and left with my luggage.

"Please, sit down." He said motioning to a chair opposite his desk.

I sat down in the wooden chair; the silence was like it had been on the car ride.

"You don't remember me do you?"

"No, I'm sorry." I said shaking my head.

"Well I didn't expect you to. It has been nine years." He said with a small smile.

"Uncle Eric!" I said in disbelief.

"Yes. You look very different yourself Lily. You seem to have grown into a fine young lady."

"Thanks." I replied.

"What are you now... sixteen?" He asked

"Yeah, " I replied.

"I am very sorry about your parents and I am sorry that I couldn't male it to the funeral. I was busy making arrangements for you, " he apologized with sadness is his eyes.

"It's okay." I replied trying to sound nonchalant.

"Yes, well." He said clearing his throat. "If you haven't already noticed, this is a Military Academy. I work and live here. I have made arrangements for you to attend school and live here, but I have asked that you be excluded from all military related activities." He explained.

'THANK GOD!' I silently cried in my head.

"Okay, " I answered, trying to hide my happiness.

"You will live in the junior dorms with the rest of the juniors. Here is your room key." He said as he handed me a small key with the number 314 printed on it.

"Your luggage has already been brought up to your dorm room," he added.

"Thanks," I said as I took the key from him.

"Oh and I am sorry but you're going to have three roommates. There was no room left for you to have your own room, " he informed me,

"That's okay. I'm fine with sharing." Having roommates isn't that bad. We could be besties. I giggled at that thought.

"A..And there is one more thing you should know, " he said, looking at me.

"What?" I asked him.

"This is an all boys academy," he stated calmly.

'What did he just say!?'

"W..Wh..What?" I blurted out.

"I know that this is a shock, but there were no other options. The boys will arrive later today, back from fall break," he stated.

" I'm sharing a room with three guys?" I asked for confirmation. Please say no. Why is this happening to me?

"Yes, I am very sorry and since this was such short notice, none of them know that you are here yet, so it will be quite a surprise for them too, " my uncle replied.

I couldn't say anything. What were you supposed to say to that? "Oh golly gee thanks!" NO! this was going to be just great. Just fucking great!

2

- -

F rancisco Lachowski as Will.

As I trudged across the campus, all I could think about were boys. Boys were running through my mind, and soon they would be running everywhere else too. I reached the junior dorm building and pulled open the glass doors that led into the lobby. Just as my uncle had said, the boys had not yet arrived, therefore resulting in an empty lobby. The lobby was nothing special. A couple couches here and there and a table there.

I made my way to the opposite end of the lobby and pressed the up button for the elevator. The doors immediately slid open and I stepped in and pushed the number three button. Reaching the top floor a bell sounded, and the doors slid open allowing me to get off.

"306, 308, 310, 312, 314." I mumbled to myself as I walked down the hall to my new dorm.

I unlocked the door and stepped inside. Upon entering, I saw four identical twin beds with dark blue sheets and dark blue comforters. Off to the right side against the wall were two desks, and through a small doorway on the left, I caught sight of what seemed to be a living room. There was a large closet, which I presumed would be shared, and four sets of drawers. One by each bed that served as a nightstand. Looking around, I found one crucial thing that was missing, a bathroom.

"There's no bathroom." I said in disbelief.

"OH MY GOD! WHAT IF IT'S A COMMUNITY BATHROOM!" I practically yelled.

Frustrated, I flopped back onto my bed and stared at the ceiling. After a good five minutes of doing absolutely nothing, I decided to get up and unpack. Of course the first thing I did was plug in my laptop so I could listen to music while unpacking.

For the next three hours, I danced around the room singing along with every song, while putting away all of my clothes and other personal items. I was in the middle of dancing to Justin Timberlake's 'Sexy Back', when the door opened.

Unfortunately for me, my music was up so loud and I was too involved with my dancing I didn't notice. Oh and because I have such wonderful luck, I wasn't just dancing a little, oh no I was dancing a lot. Everything from turns, jumps, swinging hips, arms thrown in the air, to droppin it like it's hot!

Standing in the doorway were three guys, who all had the same expression on their faces. I continued to dance around the room oblivious to its new occupants. That was until I spun around, opened my eyes, screamed, and fell flat on my ass.

I remained on the floor, blushing like an idiot, while all three guys proceeded to gawk at me. After what seemed like five hours, but in all reality had only been five seconds, I pushed myself up off the floor. As I was brushing myself off, they continued to stare.

"You're a girl." A guy that had to be at least 6'1 with brown shaggy hair and chocolate brown eyes stated.

Yep ladies and gentlemen, that was the first thing I heard out of my new roommate's mouth. DUH! What gave that away! Maybe the long hair, girlish figure, or HEY! Maybe it was the breast!

"Umm.. Yeah." I replied. What was I supposed to say!

"Why are you in our room?" The guy on the right said.

He had blonde hair and light blue eyes. He seemed to only be an inch shorter than the first guy.

"Because this is my dorm." I stated.

"But this is an all boys school!" The last one exclaimed.

He had auburn colored hair with hazel eyes and stood about as tall as the second boy.

"I know."

"So.. Then are you going to school here?" The first one questioned.

"Yeah, but I don't have to do any military activities, " I replied.

None of the guys said anymore, they just continued to stare at me. Yeah that was definitely uncomfortable. Way to make a girl feel welcome, stare a hole through her!

"Um.. Well my name's Lily," I introduced myself.

"Oh yeah! I'm Will." The guy with the shaggy brown hair stated.

"I'm Ian." The blonde said.

"And I'm Oliver." The one with auburn hair stated.

"Cool. Nice to meet yall," I said.

"Are you American?" Ian asked me.

"Yeah. How did ya know?"

"Your accent is a dead giveaway." He said smiling.

"Oh. So do you guys know if the bathroom is a community bathroom?" I asked hoping that the answer would be 'NO! Of course not! Everyone has their own private one!'

"Yeah. Each floor shares one." Will said as he sat his bags down on the bed next to mine.

"Great!"

"What's the big-. Oh." Ian said as he figured it out.

"Yeah. I'm gonna go take a shower before anyone else gets in." I said grabby one of my fluffy pink towels and heading out the door.

"HEY! Wa-." Oliver didn't get to finish his sentence. I was already out the door and halfway down the hall.

"Do you think we should have told her about the annual senior prank?" Will questioned his friends.

"I tried to tell her." Oliver said shrugging his shoulders as he proceeded to unpack.

'Alright! Where the hell is the bathroom!' I thought as I continued to walk down the endless hallway.

I had been receiving confused and shocked looks from the few boys that I had passed in the hall. I rounded a corner at the end of the hallway and found the bathroom.

'Hell yeah! Go me!' I silently cheered myself.

I pushed open the door to the bathroom and saw several showerheads on the wall. Luckily there were curtains separating each one from the other. There was a long counter with several sinks and mirrors. I stripped out of my polo, jeans, bra, and panties, and laid them, along with my towel on the counter. I stepped into the shower and pulled the curtains closed on both sides.

'Exactly what I need! A nice hot shower!' I thought to myself as I turned the knob.

Unfortunately that's not what I got. Turning the knob labeled hot, I was over come with an icy blast of water. I shrieked and jumped away from the water, slipping on the floor and landing under the ice-cold stream that was now flowing over my shivering body.

I groped the wall until I finally found the knob. With a sharp twist the torture ended. I was soaked from head to toe and I was pissed. I stormed out of the shower wrapping my towel around myself and grabbing my clothes, I stomped into the hallway.

There were quite a few more boys than there had been before and that every last pair of eyes were focused directly on me. Of course I had to be stupid and only have a towel on, a short towel at that. All noise that was previously in the hallway ceased. I gripped my towel tighter, bent my head to the floor, and hurried back to my room as quick as possible.

Reaching my dorm, I quickly stepped inside and closed the door. That's when I exploded.

"WHY THE HELL DIDN'T YOU TELL ME THAT THERE ISN'T ANY HOT WATER?"

Oliver looked up from his suitcase that he had been unpacking. He stopped with a green shirt clutched in his hand, mouth agape. I waited a few seconds before remembering that I was still just in a towel.

"HELLO!"

"Um.. I tried to tell you but you already left."

"So is there never hot water?"

"No, the seniors always shut off all the hot water to all the other dorms after every break, for a few days." He explained to me, what completely sounded like an idiotic, immature prank!

"What's all the shouting about?" Will asked as he walked into the room followed by Ian.

They both stopped and stared at me. I swear, these boys seriously need to learn some manners! They just won't stop staring!

"STOP STARING!" I yelled at all three of them, since I had just noticed that once again Oliver was staring at me.

Their gazes immediately dropped to the floor.

"There is no way I am taking a cold shower for the next few days."

"It's either that or no shower." Will said smirking at me.

"Wanna bet?" I replied hotly.

"What do you plan on doing about it?" Will asked.

"Where are the senior dorms?" I asked him.

"It's the building to the right. Why?" Oliver asked.

"Oh, no reason." I replied.

I grabbed my clothes and walked into the closet, closing the door behind me and changed. I made sure to grab an extra pair of clothes this time. I slipped my pink flip-flops back on and walked out towel and bathroom products in hand.

"Where are you going?" Ian asked as I headed for the door.

"To take a hot shower." Was all I said.

I walked determinedly down the hall and into the elevator. Crossing the lobby, I caught the gaze of a few boys lounging around. I kept my gaze straight ahead as I walked out the door and into the senior dorm building.

'I will NOT take cold showers!'

I made my way down the first floor hallway, turned the corner, and pushed open the bathroom door. It was exactly the same as the junior dorms. Once again I stripped out of my clothes and laid them and my towel on the counter. I stepped into the shower, closed the curtains, and turned the knob. Hot water! All of my muscles relaxed as the hot water pelted down onto me and rolled down my skin.

After a long, hot, well-deserved, shower, I stepped out and wrapped my towel around my body. I began to sing softly James Blunt's 'Goodbye My Lover,' steadily growing louder and louder as I came to the chorus. The door opened and I could hear voices coming towards me. I immediately stopped singing.

"Did you hear someone singing?"

"Yeah I did."

"Well whoever he is sounds like the don't ask, don't tell type."

They all laughed as they rounded the corner. I grabbed my clothes and ducked around the wall and crouched to the ground.

'SHIT! How am I supposed to get out of here?' I asked myelf.

"Where is he?"

"I don't know, he couldn't have left, we would have seen him."

"What if he's hiding in here trying to look at us?"

"All right! That's it! Whoever you are, you better come out of hiding!" One of the voices demanded.

"No! I am so dead!' I told myself.

"Come out now or we will make this year a living hell for you!" Another one threatened.

'Psh! Yeah! I don't think that it could get any worse.' I thought to myself as I rolled my eyes. 'Maybe I should just get this over with.'

I took a deep breath and stood up holding onto my towel. Their backs were to me, so I gave a small cough to get their attention. They all spun around looking like they were going to kill me. Their expressions quickly changed to shock. I was about two feet away from three guys that were all easily over six feet tall. One had black hair, the second one had blonde, and the last one was flaming red.

"Where's the guy?" The blonde asked me.

'There is no guy." I replied.

"But we heard someone singing."

"Um.. that was me." I said lowering my gaze to the ground.

"Are you one of the guy's sister or girlfriend?" The guy with black hair questioned.

"No." I answered. Girlfriends are allowed here?

"Then why are you here?" One of them asked as he stared at me.

"I go here now." I replied.

"You can't go here. This is an all boys academy." The guy with the black hair stated.

"Well now it's an all boys and one girl academy." I stated sarcastically growing tired of their questions.

"Even if you DID go here, you don't look like a senior," he added.

"I'm not. I'm a junior, " I replied. What is this, Twenty Questions?

"Then why are you in our dorms?" He asked as he studied me.

"Because you obviously think that it's funny to turn off all the hot water, and I wasn't gonna take a cold shower." I said crossing my arms over my chest.

"Maybe we should keep the hot water off all year, if we get to see this everyday." The red head boy stated smirking, as he looked me up and down.

"PERV!" I yelled as I hurried into a stall clothes in hand to change.

When I had finished changing, I stepped out of the stall to find the bathroom completely empty. I walked out into the hallway to not only see the previous three guys but what looked like the entire senior dorm! They were all lined up against the walls. I made my way down the hall as fast as possible. On my way, I received several wolf whistles and shouts. I pushed out of the building and headed back towards my own dorm, away from the boys and towards even more of them.

My life is so great.

3

P ic is Tyler Hoechlin as Liam Kalsen

Once I was safely inside of my dorm room, I flopped down onto my bed and closed my eyes, enjoying the silence. Unfortunately for me, my silence lasted about three seconds before it was shattered by several loud voices.

'God! Can I not get one minute of peace around here?'

"Oh hey Lily. We didn't think you would be back yet. Where did you go?" Will said as he walked through the door followed by Ian, Oliver, and four guys that I didn't know.

"I went to the senior dorms." I said sitting up on my bed.

"Why?" He asked.

"To take a hot shower," I answered.

"You took a shower in the senior dorms?" One of the new guys asked in amazement. He had shaggy jet-black hair and dull gray eyes.

"Um.. Yeah. Who are you?" I asked waving my hand at the small group of boys, that were staring at me like they had never saw a girl in their entire life.

"Oh sorry. This is Cal, Dave, John and Jason." Will said pointing to each guy.

Jason was the one with jet-black hair and gray eyes. He stood 6'0 tall and had a muscular build. Dave had light blonde hair that was almost white, with piercing blue eyes. He was taller than Cal at 6'3 and had a lean yet muscular build. John and Jason were identical twins. They both had dark brown hair with chocolate colored eyes. They were the same height as Cal and they both had a mischievous grin on their face.

"So are you all juniors too?"

"Yeah we all live across the hall." Dave answered.

"If you ever get lonely, you can just come on over." Jason said winking at me.

"Shut up!" Will said elbowing him in the ribs.

"Sorry mate, didn't know she was already yours." He said holding up his hands in defense and smiling.

"She's not mine." Will mumbled to the floor.

"Good, then she's up for grabs!" Jason said happily.

I couldn't believe this! They were talking about me like I was a piece of property! I knew guys talked about girls, but hello, I was standing right in front of them!

"Excuse me, but I am nobody's and I am not 'up for grabs!' I'm a person not a thing!" I exclaimed.

"Calm down love, I didn't mean it like that. Bloody hell," Jason apologized.

"First don't call me love and you just said bloody hell. What are you British?"

"Actually, I am British. We are in Londo, love, " he teased.

"Oh yeah., I forgot. Hey! Stop calling me that!" I glared at him.

"Sorry love, habit." He said with a smirk.

I rolled my eyes and went back over to my bed. My eyes started to droop and I could fill the jet lag starting to kick in. I fell asleep curled up on top of my bed, not even thinking about school starting the next day.

The next morning the first thing I heard was a loud buzzing sound coming from my alarm clock. I groaned and rolled over slapping the off button and climbing out of bed. The guys were all still asleep, how I don't know, but it didn't bother me.

I walked slowly to the closet and opened the closet. Inside I found a uniform with a not attached to it.

Lily,

Here is your uniform. Please wear this every school day.

-Uncle Eric

I held up my new uniform to look at it. It consisted of a gray skirt, thankfully not too short, and a maroon polo shirt. I shut the closet door and put on a pair of shorts under my skirt and then pulled the polo over my head.

I stepped out of the closet and looked into the mirror. 'Not bad.' I thought looking at my reflection.

"Not bad." Ian said from behind me.

"Thanks." I said as I walked over and grabbed my make-up bag.

I applied some light powder, blush, eye shadow, lip-gloss and mascara. I liked make-up, what can I say, I'm girlie but trust me I'm no ditz or slut. By the time I had finished, all of the boys were up and were slowly getting ready. Not wanting to see anymore than I wanted to, I stepped out into the hallway and waited.

The boys came out all dressed in identical uniforms, kacki pants, with a white button up shirt and maroon tie. 'DAMN! They look hot!' I thought glancing at each of them. Across the hall, the door opened and Cal, Dave, John and Jason stepped out.

"You want to get some breakfast before school?" Will asked me.

"Sure, lead the way." I smiled at him.

When we reached the cafeteria, the boys showed me how to buy food on my account, and invited me to sit at their table. I felt awkward. I didn't know these people very well and I could feel the eyes of every person in the room on me. There weren't that many people down here. I guess they all decided to sleep in as much as possible.

The boys talked amongst themselves seeming to forget I was even there. That was until another guy approached the table. My Lord! He made my knees go weak even when I was sitting! He had coal black hair with a few stray pieced hanging in front of his ice blue eyes. He smiled at me and held out his hand.

"Liam Kalsen," the hot guy intoduced himself.

"Lily Daniels." I said extending my hand and smiling. You have to smile when a hot guy introduces himself to you. Guys get attracted to that, right?

He took it and kissed it lightly before letting it drop to my side. Cheesy I know, but damn he was hot! I practically melted. I hadn't even noticed that all the guys at my table had stopped talking and were staring, well more of glaring at Liam.

"It was nice to meet you Lily, hope to see you around," Liam said.

"You too." I said as he walked away.

I returned my gaze back to the table only to be met by the glares of the boys. They looked pissed. I don't know why, maybe they were all gay and wanted him for themselves.No way, he was mine and I don't share! I should have peed on him, like what dogs do, to mark my territory and show them he was mine.

"Lily, you shouldn't talk to him." Will stated.

"Why not?" I asked.

"He's a bloody wanker that's why!" One of the twins, I couldn't tell which one, yelled.

"Okay, one, I don't know what wanker is so I'm just going to ignore that, and two, he seems really hot, I mean nice. Why do you guys hate him?" I stated.

"Trust us, he's not nice, he has a reputation."

"Of what?" I said crossing my arms. "He can't exactly be a player unless he's gay." I argued.

"Well he is, he's dated about every girl in the area." Will answered..

"Whatever." I waved them off.

"Fine. What classes do you have?" Oliver asked.

"I don't know."

"Well, look at your schedule."

"I didn't get one." I said getting nervous. I didn't want to screw up on my first day.

"Oh yeah! Sorry I forgot too give it to you." Will said smiling sheepishly as he handed me a small piece of paper.

"Thanks," I thanked him.

I looked down at my schedule and went through all of my classes.

Period 1: Literature- Mr. Callen

Period 2: Pre-Calculus-Mr. Fen

Period 3: Gym- Coach Delton

Period 4: Lunch

Period 5: History-Mr. Horsh

Period 6: Chemistry-Mr. Gale

Period 7: Military Training- General McKain

Each class will last one hour with the exception of lunch, which will last for forty-five minutes.

"Uh, I think there's been a mistake. I was told that I didn't have to do any military stuff." I stated.

"Oh that's probably just a typo you can talk with General McKain when you get there." Will said nonchalantly

'I'm sure he'll understand he's my uncle!' I thought to myself no linger worrying about it.

"So do any of yall have Mr. Callen for Literature first period?" I asked hoping at least one would say yes.

"I do." Ian said.

"Me too." Oliver chimed in.

"Count me in." Dave said with a grin.

"Thank God!" I said, letting out a sigh. Now I wouldn't get lost or walk in without knowing anyone.

"We should all get to our classes, we only have five minutes until class starts." Will said standing up.

"Alright I'll see the rest of you all later."

"Bye!" They all echoed as they took off in different directions.

"Would the lady like an escort to her class?" Dave said, grinning like an idiot as he held out his arm.

"Yes, she would." I replied in mock humor as I latched my arm through his.

Dave, Oliver and Ian all led me to our first class Literature. I was so happy that my first class was Literature. I rocked at this class. Give me a book I'll read it and tell you everything about it! We walked into the classroom and all noise ceased to exist. All eyes fell on me and what looked like my own personal bodyguards.

"You must be Miss Daniels." A man that looked to be in about his mid thirties with buzzed brown hair and glasses said glancing at a piece of paper.

"Yeah." I said.

"Well, welcome to Wilmington. I'm Mr. Callen."

"Thanks."

He gave me a kind welcoming smile and then his eyes fell on my arm. It was still linked with Dave's. I blushed and pulled my arm from his. He seemed to get the picture and thought it was funny. He gave me an over dramatic pout and walked towards a group of four desks next to each other. Oliver, Ian and I followed. All the other boys seemed to be in a daze. Mr. Callen seemed to notice this and shook his head.

"Miss Daniels, could you please come to the front of the room and introduce yourself?" He said with a smile.

I walked to the front of the classroom and pulled down nervously on my polo. I pulled at the edge of my skirt, trying to make it longer as I noticed several pair of eyes traveling down my legs.

"Hi. I'm Lily Daniels and I'm from Kentucky." I blurted out.

What was I supposed to say? 'HI! My name's Lily like the flower and my favorite color is pink. I like spaghetti and DAMN! All of you are hot!' Not likely. I was about ready to go back to my seat when one of the boys yelled at me.

"Why are you here?" he asked.

"I go to school here now." I responded.

"This is an all boys school." Another called.

"Um.. Well yeah but-"

"Are you really from Kentucky?" Another interrupted me.

'When the flip this turn into a question and answer session?'

"It's time for class to start. You all can talk to Lily later." Mr. Callen said, saving me from having to answer.

Thank God for him! I didn't really want to tell people the real reason I was here. I didn't want to have to tell them about my parents. No more questions came my way, thankfully. At the end of class, I met up with Will and the twins who had Pre-Calculus with me along with Dave.

Let me tell you, I suck at math! That class was pure torture! Not only had it consisted of more awkward introductions and staring, but there were numbers. Numbers and I don't get along. I usually end up throwing my pencil across the room and slamming my book. I had to refrain from my pencil throwing and book slamming antics so I wouldn't appear to be crazy.

So far, both of the teachers I had met, Mr. Callen and Mr. Fen, were pretty nice and welcoming. That all changed when I got to gym. I had a feeling that Coach Delton and I were not going to get along, not one bit.

4

- -

Coach Delton was a large, tall, man. He wore a pair of dark blue gym shorts and a gray T-shirt that read 'Wilmington Military Academy' est.1921. He had graying hair cut close to his head and at the moment his eyes were narrowed into slits that made them look black. Those little black slits were glaring, at me.

"Everyone go change!" He bellowed in his deep commanding voice.

All of the boys including Will, Ian, and Oliver, whom were in my class headed towards what I guessed was the locker room. I stood were I was for two reasons. One, I didn't have a gym uniform, and two, I was not changing in a room full of boys.

"Excuse me, Coach Delton." I asked tentatively.

"What?" He growled, glaring at me.

"I don't have a uniform."

"Here." He said tossing a pair of maroon shorts and a gray shirt identical to his.

I stood there with the new uniform in hand unsure of what to do next.

"What are you waiting for? Go change!"

"Where?"

"In the locker room." He said pointing to the door that the boys had previously entered.

"I can't change in the boys locker room."

"Why not?" He growled growing irritated.

"Because I'm a girl and those are boys." I said slowly trying to make him understand that we were two VERY different species.

"Fine. Then you can wait for them to finish changing and then go in."

I walked over and leaned against the wall waiting for the boys to come out. No sooner than my back touched the wall the boys came rushing out, obviously excited to start the class. I walked in and made sure that they were all gone and then changed into my new uniform. It was big on me. I had to roll the shorts to make them a comfortable length and the shirt hung loosely on my frame. I pulled the pink hair tie off my wrist and swept my hair up into a messy ponytail.

I came out to see all of the boys running laps around the gym.

"Five laps!" Coach Delton yelled across the gym to me.

I started a quick run and easily completed my laps with the boys even though they had gotten a head start. I walked over to the coach talking to Will and stood in a group of guys waiting further instruction.

"You didn't finish your laps!" Coach Delton yelled at me.

"Yes I did."

"You started later than everyone else and you finished at the same time. That's not possible. Two more laps!" He ordered.

I gave him a glare but decided that I didn't want to get into trouble on my first day so I took off around the gym. I sprinted the two laps and made my way back into the crowd of boys. The coach seemed surprised at how quickly I had finished the laps but continued to talk.

'HA! Didn't think I was any good! That's what eleven years of volleyball, softball, and tennis does for you!'

I had tuned him out while he had been talking and was now confused when two guys started to call out names. They were picking teams and the group of guys was slowly growing smaller. Will, Ian, and Oliver had already been picked, leaving me and three other guys standing.

"Sam." The guy standing next to me went and joined his new team.

"Ron."

"Vince." The last guy standing left and joined his team leaving me alone to be picked last.

"Great. The girl." My new team captain grumbled.

"It's Lily." I shot back walking over and joining my team. Unfortunately Will, Ian, and Oliver were all on the other team.

"What are we doing?" I asked a random guy next to me.

"We're playing volleyball." He said before walking away.

'HELL YEAH! I ROCK AT THIS GAME!'

With my new re-found confidence I walked over to the small huddle and listened while the team captain talked.

"Okay. They've got some pretty good players on their team, but so do we. Everyone try and set up Mike and Travis. Oh, and keep it away from the girl, she'll screw up." He added as an afterthought as though I wasn't there.

"Excuse me?" I said becoming angry.

He looked over at me and the back to the rest of the group. "Like I said, don't pass to the girl."

"HEY! I have a name! It's Lily, and I've played volleyball since I was in first grade and I damn good!" I said putting my hand on my hip and pushing it out to the side.

When I was twelve I went through a feminist phase. I called every guy that talked to me a sexist, chauvinistic, pig. I finally got over that little phase in my life, but right now this sexist, chauvinistic, pig was bringing it out of me again.

He was about ready to retaliate when Coach Delton blew his whistle fir us to begin. I was in the back corner and let me tell you; those boys did a damn good job of keeping the ball away from me. They would rather give up the point by diving in front of me and knocking it out then to let me touch it. I was about ready to rip their heads of, but then it was my turn to serve. Finally I got to touch the ball!

I actually debated whether or not to serve it right into Rick's, the team captain, head. I decided against this not wanting to lose any more points. I tossed the ball high in the air and jumped, bringing my arm down and hitting the ball. It soared over the net with immense speed. It hit Oliver's arms and spun out of bounds. All of my teammates turned to look at me; Rick's mouth was wide open. The ball rolled back to me and I picked it up ready to serve again.

Coach Delton blew his whistle, signaling the end of the period. I walked over and stood against the wall waiting for the boys to finish changing.

My team had one 25-16. Of course the guys on my team would never admit that I was the main reason for the win, they said it was teamwork. Whatever.

The boys came out and I went in and quickly changed. Coming out I was met by Will, Ian, and Oliver. They had wide grins on their faces; they looked like a bunch of idiots.

"Where did you learn to play like that?" Ian asked as we started for the cafeteria.

"Yeah! You kicked our asses!" Oliver threw in.

"I started playing in first grade." I said shrugging my shoulders.

"Well you're bloody brilliant!" Ian said throwing his hands into the air as we entered the cafeteria.

We stood in line to get our lunch. I ended up with a hamburger and fries. They led me back to the table that we had eaten at that morning. The other guys were already there. To me it looked like they were seeing who could eat their lunch the fastest. Sitting down proved otherwise, because Will, Ian, and Oliver tore into theirs as well. It was disgusting, they chewed with their mouths open and some food was even flying out.

I picked up a fry and placed it in my mouth. EW! It was disgusting. They noticed the pained expression on my face and stopped their gorge fest.

"You going to finish your fries?" One of the twins asked me with a hopeful expression on his face. His twin's head popped around him with the same hopeful expression.

"No. You can have them." I said laughing at their expressions.

They grabbed them like they were gold and began to shovel them into their mouths.

"So who has History with Mr. Horsh next?" I asked looking around the table.

None of them raised their hands or said yes. This was not good! I was going to be in a class by myself. Plus I didn't know how to get there. I was panicking on the inside. I noticed the boys were glaring. At first I thought they were glaring at me, but then I noticed their gazes fell on what was behind me.

"I have history next period." A smooth, deep, voice said from behind me.

I turned to see who it was. I smiled like an idiot. It was Liam.

"I would be happy to escort you to class." He said smiling.

"Thanks." I replied with that stupid smile still plastered on my face.

I noticed his gaze wasn't on me. He was still smiling but he was looking past me, almost through me. He was looking at Cal. I thought that was a little weird but brushed it off when the bell rang. Liam held out his arm for me to take and I latched on, saying good-bye to the guys over my shoulder.

I didn't care if the guys were shooting dirty glares at Liam as he escorted me out of the cafeteria and down the hall to my next class. All I could think about was how pretty he was. Wait, pretty, I meant hot.

"How do you like it here so far?" He asked turning to glance at me.

"Oh, it's okay. I mean I'm not used to not having other girls around and all but yeah." I said quickly running out of words.

"You'll get used to it. It can't be all bad"

"Yeah."

Our conversation was cut short as we entered the classroom and Liam led me to the seat next to his. This was one of my best subjects, history. No worries, this would be an easy A. After the introductions the class began.

On the board Mr. Horsh wrote Early English History. Oh crap. I was great at American history but I knew squat about England's history. All I knew was that we beat them in the war and won our freedom. Liam seemed to notice the troubled look on my face and leaned over.

"Is something wrong?" He whispered.

"I don't know English history, only American!" I whispered nervously back.

"Don't worry I'll help you." He said smiling and leaning back in his seat.

I relaxed after this and listened as closely as I could, trying to soak up everything coming out of this man's mouth. This was a hard task seeing as Mr. Horsh had a very dull, boring voice. I could feel my eyelids drooping. However they popped open when I heard the words pop quiz.

Oh God! How was I going to do this? They had already had a full semester of this class and they lived here their whole lives! I was in trouble! No I was dead.

"Sir, I don't think it's fair that Lily has to take this seeing as she is new and she grew up in America." Liam said from beside me. He looked so calm and sure of himself.

"Hm.. I guess you're right Mr. Kalsen. Ms. Daniels, you are excused from today's quiz." He said as he handed out copies of the quiz.

Liam Kalsen was my new hero. That boy had just saved me from complete failure. I looked over at him and mouthed a silent thank you. Which was responded to by him smiling and running a hand through his hair. Yet again I noticed his gaze went over my head. Weird.

5

C hemistry had been simple. I had the class with all of the boys and my lab partner was Will. Well, it had been simple before John and Jason almost blew up the lab by adding two chemicals together on "accident." Now all that was left of the day was Military Training, which of course I would get out of from my Uncle.

All of the junior boys had changed into what I guessed was their training clothes. I was still in my school uniform as we walked across the campus towards the obstacle course. All I could think of was getting back to my dorm and taking a shower before the boys got back. Oh and My Boy Lollipop which was now officially stuck in my head.

Reaching the obstacle course I noticed Uncle Jack standing in military fashion looking rather stern. I had never seen this side of him, he was always Uncle Jack the one who when I was little put me on his shoulders and spun me around until I couldn't walk straight. That was before he moved to London.

We were all lined up in a straight line awaiting orders, in my part waiting to be dismissed. My Uncle walked down the line and stopped at the end. Turning sharply on his heal he yelled.

"Seventy Five push ups!"

All of the boys immediately dropped to the ground and began. This left me standing around looking out of place. Not that I wasn't already standing out enough. I stepped out of line and walked down to where Uncle Jack was standing.

"Hi." I said as I stopped in front of him.

"Hello Lily."

"Umm I think there is something wrong with my schedule." I said showing him where it said military training.

"Yes this does seem to be a mistake." He said furrowing his brow.

"So I can just go to my dorm now?" I said already putting my schedule away.

"Yes, you can go. I am sorry about this mistake."

"It's okay." I replied heading back towards my dorm.

After a long hot shower, in my actual dorm building this time I made my way back to the room. Obviously the boys were still training and I had some time to myself. Finally no boys, no noise just me, myself and I. I got on my laptop and selected My Boy Lollipop from my play list. Might as well play it if it was stuck in my head.

Of course if there was music playing, I was going to partake in one of my favorite past times; dancing like a crazy person. Of course twirling around the room was not enough for me. My bed caught my eye. It was too late, I was on top of my bed jumping and signing. My wonderful rendition of Millie Small was interrupted by a knock on the door.

"Forgot your keys." I said opening the door.

"Actually I have mine, but this isn't my room." Liam said with a wide smile.

"Oh. Sorry I thought you were one of my roommates."

"No they all opted to take a shower first."

"You wanna come in?" I asked opening the door wider.

"Sure." He said as he sauntered in and sat down on my bed.

"So…" I said looking for something interesting to say. "How was training?" I asked.

"Fine. The usual." He replied shortly. Big help, thanks.

He sat there smiling at me, not saying a word. Just staring.

"It's nice to have a girl around here." He stated.

"Um.. Thanks?" I answered not sure if he was complimenting me or not.

I found myself staring into Liam's ice blue eyes. Somehow they didn't hold the same weak-kneed power they had the first time I had seen them. They were pretty yes, but it just wasn't there.

"What is he doing in here?" Came a voice from the doorway.

Our gazes fell from each other and rested on Will who was standing in the doorway. WOW! I had that weak-kneed feeling. It wasn't from Liam, it was from Will. He was in a pair of shorts and nothing more. A few water droplets clung to his bare chest that had dropped from his wet hair.

I averted my gaze away from him and to the floor.

"I was just visiting Lily." Liam said getting up from my bed. "But I have to go now. I'll see you around Lily."

"Bye." I replied quietly, my eyes still glued to the floor.

Will watched him as he left the room, then turned back to me.

"What was he doing in here?" He asked again.

"Like he said, he was just visiting."

"Lily, do you remember what we told you at breakfast about him?" He asked walking over and grabbing a white T-shirt from the closet and slipping it on.

"Yeah so?" I retorted. It was much easier to look at him when he was dressed.

"You let him in after what we told you about him?" He asked in disbelief.

"Well so far I've seen nothing wrong with him! He's a nice guy." I said standing from my bed.

"That's how he is, until he gets what he wants then dumps the girl." He said in a softer tone.

"Whatever." I said pushing past him out the door and heading towards the cafeteria.

I was in the elevator and the doors were closing. Unfortunately Will made it inside right before they shut on him. I crossed my arms and focused on a the shiny, metal doors.

"Look Lily, I just don't want what happened to the other girls to happen to you."

"What did he kill them or something?" I tossed back sarcastically.

"No." He said sighing.

"Then what did he do?"

"He broke their hearts. He goes out with girls and shows them off, like a trophy. They're always so happy to be with 'The Liam Kalsen' until he cheats on them with the next girl."

"And this is a proven fact, not just some rumor some idiot made up?" I said looking at him as the elevator doors slid open.

"He's had 7 girlfriends in the past nine months, that's almost a girl a month."

"Really?"

"Yeah."

Both of us walked off the elevator and walked across the campus to the cafeteria. It was colder than I expected. I was only wearing a pair of jeans and a pink tee. I hugged my arms around myself as I walked.

I felt Will's arm droop around my shoulder and pull me into his body when he noticed I was cold. I looked up to see him smiling. I smiled back as we entered the cafeteria. His arm was still around me when we walked through the doors. We got some disapproving looks from the few teachers and he slid his arm off me.

I ducked my head in embarrassment and quickly got my dinner from the line. All of the other guys were already at the table and they seemed to be having a burping contest. Oh what fun! John let out an earth-shattering burp as soon as I sat down.

"And the winner is... JOHN!" Cal exclaimed in a loud voice.

"What do I win?" John asked looking around the table.

"Um.. In don't know. How about a kiss from Lily?" His twin suggested raising his eyebrows at me.

"Well..." I said stalling. Will almost spit out his drink.

"Yeah?" John asked hopefully.

"Nope." I said as I took a bite out of my turkey sandwich and smiling.

"No fair!" He said pouting and crossing his arms.

"That's what you get when you act like a caveman." I said sticking out my tongue.

"I like acting like a caveman." John stated releasing another large belch.

"Whatever." I said smiling as I stood up.

"Where are you going?" Will asked looking up at me.

"To take a shower." I said over my shoulder. "And no you can't come John." I said before the words could get out of his mouth.

His mouth closed and formed into a pout. I laughed walking back towards the dorm building. Maybe living with all guys wouldn't be as bad as I first thought it would be. Then again if I had to deal with daily burping contest I wasn't sure if I would survive.

6

Do you know how good a nice hot shower can make you feel? DAMN GOOD! I felt clean, refreshed and happy. I as dressed in purple and white plaid pajama pants with a light purple tank. I stepped out of the shower room and saw a fcw guys heading in.

"Are you taking a shower now?" A guy with black hair asked me hopefully.

"Nope, just finished." I replied flashing him a smile and walking down the hall.

"Damn." I heard him mutter under his breath.

Was that the only thing on these boys mind? I think it was official, I was the center of their worlds. Wow! That's funny. Hmm.. Queen Lily does have a nice ring to it. I returned to my dorm room to find all of my roommates lounging around doing absolutely nothing. I walked over and flopped down onto Will's bed were he was lying.

"Well ya'll are boring." I said.

"What?" Will said sitting up to make room for me to stretch out my legs.

"Is this all ya'll do? Sit around and do nothing."

"We're tired. WE had training." Ian whined.

"Be a man. Suck it up." I said jumping to my bed.

"Well if you're so smart then what do you think we should do?" Oliver asked.

"Hm..." I said putting my finger to my lips as if I was thinking.

"What?" They all asked.

"I GOT IT! Go get the other guys and bring 'em back here!"

"Okay, calm down." Oliver said holding his hands up in front of him.

A minute later they came back followed by the other four boys.

"What do you want?" Cal asked running his hand through his black hair.

"We're gonna play truth or dare." I said crossing my legs in front of me."

"Are you serious?" Jason stated.

"Of course! Plus this lets us get to know each other better." I said waving my hand in the air. "Sit down."

After a minute of complaining and grumbling they all sat down two to a bed. Will sat down on my bed with me, the twins were on one bed, Cal and Dave on another, and Oliver and Ian on the last one.

"Okay. Who starts?" Will asked.

"ME! Ladies first." I said sticking my tongue out at him.

"Fine, go."

"Um.. DAVE! Truth or dare?"

"Dare." He said bravely.

This boy had no idea what he had gotten himself into. I was known for coming up with the most embarrassing dares there ever was. One time I actually made this guy from my old school strip down to his boxers and put on some makeup and then sing girls just want to have fun while everyone else took pictures. Needless to say those pictures didn't stay private very long.

"Are you sure?" I said trying to give him a second chance.

"Yeah. Just hurry up."

"Fine. I tried to let you out of it. So don't come crying to me."

"Just tell me what I have to do." He said rolling his eyes.

"Okay. Hold on. I'll be right back." I said getting up and heading towards my closet.

I rummaged through my clothes until I found exactly what I had been looking for. I came out with my hands behind my back and an evil grin on my face.

"Oh Dave." I said in a sing song voice.

"Wh-" He stopped mid sentence when he saw what I had pulled from behind my back.

I was holding a short white skirt with a pink halter-top. In my other hand I held a pair of black stilettos. The look on his face was almost enough to make me call off the dare. Almost. Short white Hollister skirt 20 dollars, pink halter top 15 dollars, black stilettos, 25 dollars, Dave's expression, priceless.

"NO WAY!" He yelled at me.

"It's either that or the consequence."

"Consequence!" He shouted.

"You have to give Cal a lap dance." I said laughing.

"HE'S DOING THE DARE!" Cal yelled scooting away from him.

"Fine." He said taking the clothes and walking into the closet to change.

Five minutes later he emerged not as Dave, but as Davy. He looked like he was going to throttle me, but right then I was too busy trying not to fall off the bed from laughing.

"Guess you're not the only girl in school anymore!" John roared with laughter.

"Shut up!" Dave snapped. "Can I change back now?" He pleaded with me.

"Yeah sure. But only if you promise never to wear my clothes again!"

"Promise." He said stomping back into the closet.

"You are the meanest person I have ever met." He said to me once he came out in his normal clothes.

"Consider yourself lucky. I was going to make you give Cal a lap dance as part of the dare but I decided not to since it was your first time." I said hitting his arm.

"My turn." Dave said sitting back down in his spot. "Lily truth or dare?"

"Truth." I said smiling.

"Okay, are you a virgin?"

"Yes. I mumbled."

"Really? Cal interjected.

"Yeah! What you think I sleep around or something?"

"No."

"Whatever. My turn again."

"Will, truth or dare." I said turning to face him.

"Seeing what you did to Dave, I think I'm going to say truth."

"Smart man." I said smiling. "Why don't you like Liam?"

"I already told you." He said heatedly.

"Answer the question."

"He uses girls."

I knew this wasn't the only reason he didn't like Liam, but I decided not to push the matter further. We continued to play for an hour. In a an hour we had somehow managed to find out that the twins dated the same girl without telling her, Ian had to sing 'Like a Virgin', Oliver screamed like a little girl when I waxed one of his legs, and Cal had his blankie until he was twelve. It was all fun, until it came to be my turn again.

'Truth." I said when Will asked me.

"Why did you come here?"

This was the one question I had been avoiding since the day I set foot on the campus. I hadn't told anyone. They all just assumed that I was here for whatever reason they had come up with in their minds. I couldn't tell them that I was here because my parents had died. I wasn't ready to tell them yet. I didn't want pity.

"Well, I'm tired I said stretching and standing up."

"Lily answer the question." Will said.

"Sorry, I'm tired and we have school tomorrow so I'm going to bed." I glanced at Dave and Cal and they got up from my bed.

"You have to answer the question."

"Sleeping." I said crawling under my covers and closing my eyes.

"We should probably get back to our room." Cal said as he, the twins, and Dave left.

"Lily." Will said trying to pry me out from under the covers.

"No." I said pulling them over my head.

"Come on Lily." He said pulling them back down.

"Not now Will." I said shooting him a glare.

"Fine." He said giving up and crawling into his bed next to mine.

Oliver and Ian had already gotten into their beds and I could hear the quiet snores coming from Ian. Will snapped off his bedside lamp and filled the room with darkness. I felt bad for snapping at him, but I wasn't ready. I didn't know if I would ever be ready to share my dark secret.

7

R ain is a terrible awful thing. It was raining as I saw out the window when I had gotten up to get ready for school. Rain somehow seemed to fit my mood today. I still felt guilty for snapping at Will and it didn't help that he was the first one up after me this morning. It also didn't help that he looked adorably sexy with his bed head and sleepy eyes. Damn hormones. I was dressed and ready to leave before Ian had even gotten up. Oliver and Will were still lazily walking around trying to find were they had thrown their clothes the day before.

I slipped out of the room without being noticed, or so I hoped. I didn't want to face Will. What if he asked me the question again? I couldn't avoid him forever but right now I definitely could. I pulled on my gray jacket that I had grabbed on my way out and put my hood up as I stepped out into the rain.

I quickly made my way across the campus and into the cafeteria. Pulling my hood off of my head I ran my fingers through my hair. Looking around I noticed that the cafeteria was empty except for a few boys here and there with books open trying to finish homework they had forgotten to do. I walked to the nonexistent line and grabbed a bagel and some orange juice.

I wasn't hungry; rain had that effect on me. Although I would kill for some chocolate right about now.

I sat down at my empty table, which was usually filled with noisy, rowdy boys. I ate my bagel alone and rested my head on my hand as I looked around the cafeteria. I caught sight of a figure heading for my table. It was Liam.

"Good morning." He said sitting down in the chair next to me. That was where Will usually sat.

"Morning." I replied halfheartedly.

"Are you feeling alright?" He asked concerned.

"Oh. Yeah, sorry. I just don't like the rain, it brings me down."

"It can't be that bad."

"Trust me it can."

"Well life's not about waiting for the storm to pass. It's about learning to dance in the rain." He quoted.

A smile spread across my lips as I sat up.

"Mr. Poetic aren't we?" I replied.

"Ah my dear, you have no idea."

"Really."

He gave me a smug smile. "I was surprised to actually see you alone. You always seemed to be surrounded by your new bodyguards."

"Yeah. I guess I am."

"I've been meaning to talk to you alone." He said becoming serious.

"Really? What about?"

"I wanted to tell you something."

"What?"

"Not here or now. It seems that your bodyguards have found you." He said motioning towards the group of seven guys approaching.

"Great." I mumbled.

"Meet me in the library at seven tonight." He whispered before standing and walking away as the group arrived at the table.

No sooner then his butt had left the seat; Will replaced him. He had that look in his eye as he glared at Liam's retreating figure.

"Oh get over it will you." I spat at him. Great add that to my guilt list.

"Why did you leave this morning?" He asked turning to face me.

"I was really hungry." I lied.

"Oh." He looked a little upset that I hadn't waited for him. God this boy was good at the guilt trip.

My first two classes went on without any trouble and then I got to Gym. As I waited for the boys to finish changing, I felt a sharp pain in my stomach. Oh God! Please not now! I rushed into the locker rooms as soon as the last boy had come out. Great. I had been visited by every girls least favorite Aunt. Aunt Flow. After taking care of that little problem and changing I walked out and ran my laps. This time I made sure he knew how many I had run.

"Today were going to play basketball." Coach Delton announced.

Today was so not my day. Basketball was my worst sport by far. He picked Will and Oliver to be team captains. Oliver had first pick and selected Ian. Will looked in my direction and smiled. I shook my head no trying to warn him of my horrible skills, but he didn't pay any attention.

"Lily." He said. I walked over dejectedly and crossed my arms in front of me.

"I suck." I whispered to him as Oliver selected his next pick.

"You're good at volleyball."

"That doesn't mean I'm good at basketball."

"Greg." He said picking his next player.

"Stop being modest." He said throwing a smile at me.

This boy really didn't know when to take a hint.

"Fine. When we lose don't blame my horrible skills, blame your failure to read body language."

He laughed as he selected the next player whom was called Alan.

The teams had been picked six on each team. I had begged Will to leave me on the bench but he refused. The minute the game started, I started sucking. Will passed me the ball and I dropped it. I'm amazing aren't I. Will looked at me in disbelief.

"I TOLD YOU!" I shouted at him as he ran down the court chasing the other team that had acquired that dropped ball.

I finally convinced Will to bench me. It took him six dropped passes that I made to finally do it. You think he would have done it the first time. I walked over and lay down on the bench as my replacement got up and joined the game. He wasn't very good, but he was better than I was. I closed my eyes and placed the palms of my hands over my stomach trying to ease the cramps.

As soon as Gym ended and I had changed I walked out with Will, Ian, and Oliver. We were headed towards the cafeteria. I broke away from the group and headed back towards my dorm.

"Where are you going?" Oliver asked turning around causing the other guys to stop.

"I just need to get something." Yeah, some midol! I said still walking.

"I'll come with you." Will said jogging up beside me.

"You don't have to." I said not wanting him to know what I was going back for, but most of all not wanting to give him the opportunity to question me again.

"It's fine. I don't mind." He said draping and arm around my shoulder and giving me a friendly squeeze.

I smiled. Will was a great guy. How could I snap at him like I did? Especially with those gorgeous brown eyes, and that cute smile, and the way his hair looks in the morning. DAMN HORMONES! I cursed in my head.

He finally removed his arm once we reached our building and we got into the elevator. We arrived at our room and walked in. I rummaged through one of my drawers until I found the box containing my relief and quickly swallowed them.

"Lily what was that?" Will asked seriously.

"What? Nothing."

"You just took some pills."

"Yeah." Great now he thought I was a pill popping druggie.

"What were they."

"Nothing."

"Lily are you on drugs?"

"No."

"Then what were they?"

"Nothing!"

"Lily!"

"Damn! It was Midol! I'm on my period!" I screamed without realizing what I had screamed. Damn hormones.

"Oh." Was all he said looking at the floor his cheeks red.

"Sorry about snapping at you. It's not your fault."

"I shouldn't have asked." He said looking up.

"No. It's good. It shows that you care." I said giving him a small smile.

"Ready for lunch?" He asked.

"Yeah. Do you think they'll have any chocolate?"

"For our sakes I hope they do." He said laughing as we walked out of the room.

The rest of my day had been good. The rain had stopped along with my cramps; they DID have chocolate, and Will never brought up the previous night's question. Right now Will, Ian, Oliver and I were all in our room finishing our homework. I had just finished when I looked over at the clock and saw the glowing red letters. It was 7:30! I was supposed to meet Liam in the library thirty minutes ago. I jumped up and grabbed my jacket running for the door.

"Where you going?" Ian asked looking up from his Math homework.

"Uh. Just getting some air." I yelled slamming the door.

As soon as the elevator doors slid open I ran outside, heading in the direction of the library. Liam was going to kill me! It sounded like he had something really important to tell me. I burst through the library doors too find it empty. Empty except for Liam sitting at one of the long wooden tables leaning back in his chair.

"You're late."

8

"Liam, I am so sorry! I got caught up in my homework and lost track of time and- "

"It's okay." He said cutting me off. "Sit down." He said motioning to the chair across from him.

I walked over and slid into the chair opposite of him and rested my elbows on the table, with my chin in my hands.

"So what did you want to tell me?"

"Right, that." He said letting the front two legs of the chair drop back onto the ground.

"As I'm sure you've noticed this school is filled with boys and boys alone, except for you."

"Yeah."

"Well I was wondering if I could tell you something, but you have to promise NOT to tell anyone. Okay?"

"Yeah. You can tell me. I won't tell anyone."

"I can trust you?"

"Liam. I swear I won't tell a soul." I said in a serious tone.

He drew in a deep breath and held it before letting it go. He closed his eyes and fidgeted with his hands that were folded on top of the table. He was making me nervous. Was something wrong? Had he done something bad, illegal?

"I'm gay." He said looking up waiting for my reaction.

I was shocked! Liam wasn't the type of guy I had pegged as being gay. Maybe I needed to get my gay-dar fixed. I didn't know what to say. I was silent for a moment until he spoke.

"So..."

"I...I.. Well I never suspected you of being gay."

"I hoped not. I don't exactly want that to get out. Especially around here."

"I won't tell anyone." I realized how hard this must have been for him. "Have you told anyone else about it?"

"No. Not even my parents. You're the only one that knows."

I couldn't believe he would tell me of all people. He barely even knew me, and here he was confessing his deepest darkest secrets. I felt bad knowing that I was keeping my secret from him, after he just confessed his to me.

"Why me?" I asked confused.

"I thought that out of anyone you would be the most understanding."

"Why?"

"If I had come out to any of my other friends they would have called me a faggot or wouldn't talk to me again. Then the whole school would know."

"There's nothing wrong with being gay." I said placing my hand on top of his.

"Apparently to some people it is."

"I am curious however, because Will said that you had dated a lot of girls and then dumped them after you had gotten what you wanted from them."

"I did date a lot of girls, but I NEVER did anything with them. They were just a cover up."

"I guess it's hard being around all these guys?"

"As hard as it is for you, I'm guessing." He said with a smile.

"Yeah it is." I smiled myself.

Liam wasn't a bad person. He was just a person with a secret. Like me.

"Lily."

I turned towards the door to where the voice had come from. Will was standing there. He looked angry and hurt. I followed his gaze and found that it was focused on Liam's and my hands. Mine was still lying on top of his. I quickly pulled it away.

"Will I-"

I didn't get to finish. He turned and walked out the door leaving Liam and I behind.

"You should probably go talk to him." Liam said standing from his seat when I stood.

"I know, don't worry I won't tell anyone." I reassured him.

"I know. Now go get him." He said giving me a nudge towards the door.

I stumbled outside and looked around. Will was nowhere to be seen. It was dark now and I probably couldn't see him even if he was around. I quickly walked backed to my dorm, hoping he would be there.

"Where's Will?" I asked when I walked into the room.

"Don't know." Oliver said not looking up from his homework he was still working on.

"Ian?" I asked hopefully.

"Haven't seen him since he left to look for you."

Great. This was just perfect! I had no clue where Will was, and I knew he was angry and thought that I had left to go hook up with Liam. He was so wrong in so many ways. I changed and crawled under my covers, facing Will's empty bed. It was still empty when I fell asleep.

I awoke the next morning hoping to find Will asleep in his bed so I could talk to him about what had happened. Unfortunately I wasn't that lucky. His bed was still empty and untouched, the same way it had been last night.

I dragged myself from my bed and walked into the closet and closed the doors. I slowly changed into my uniform. When I stepped out Ian and Oliver were already up. Will was still no where to be found. The boys were already changed, Ian's shirt slightly wrinkled from lying on the floor all night.

"Ready to go down for breakfast?" Oliver asked opening the door.

"No. You guys go ahead. I'll catch you later."

"You sure?" Ian asked already halfway out the door, obviously hungry.

"Yeah, go. I know you're hungry." I replied with a tired smile.

"Okay. See you later."

"Bye."

They both walked out and closed the door behind them. It was weird. The room was completely silent. It didn't seem right without the sound of the guys. I wasn't hungry; my stomach was too full with guilt to be hungry. Wait. Why did I feel guilty? It's not my fault that Will jumps to conclusions!

With this fresh notion in my mind I walked out into the hallway and slammed the door. I was angry. How dare he make me feel guilty over something I hadn't done.

I didn't bother going to breakfast. I didn't even want to see his face right about now. I flopped down on a plush brown couch in the empty lobby. After five minutes of sitting in complete silence I checked my cell phone and realized that class started in four minutes. I gathered my books and headed out the door towards Literature. Which thankfully Will was not in.

"Why didn't you come to breakfast this morning?" Dave asked as I slid into the seat next to him

"I wasn't hungry." I replied shortly, seeing as Mr. Callen had begun class.

Literature had ended far too soon for me. Why? Because this meant that I had my next class with Will and it was Pre-cal. Great, math just had to be thrown into this to add to the torture. When I walked into the classroom with Ian, Oliver, and Dave, I noticed that there were only three empty seats near Will. I sat down at the first empty desk across the room from him. I gained three weird looks from the other three boys. I ignored them pretending to be focused on my open notebook. Of course the guys that were sitting around me were ecstatic that I wasn't surrounded by my bodyguards and took this as the perfect opportunity to talk to me.

"Hi. I'm Quinton." A boy with light brown hair stated as he stuck his hand out for me to shake.

"Lily." I replied taking his hand.

"I know." He said with a smile. "Everyone knows who you are."

Okay can we say creepy? I know that I'm the only girl in a monstrous school of boys but come on! Didn't they have anything better to talk about than me? I gave him another quick smile before returning my attention to Mr. Fen.

"Hey Lily." I heard Quinton whisper.

"Yeah." I whispered trying to sound polite as possible. This guy was annoying.

"I was wondering if you wanted to go out some time?"

Was he serious? I had just met this kid literally three seconds ago and he wants to go out with me. Definitely a nut job.

"Um.. I'm not really doing the dating thing right now." I replied.

"Oh. Well maybe some other time."

"Right." I said dismissing him and focusing on the impossible problem on the board.

We played basketball in gym again. Unfortunately we had to be on the same teams. This meant I was still on Will's. Luckily he was smart enough to sit me out the entire time today. However part of me thought that he had done this out of spite.

Lunch. I couldn't sit at the same table with him. I just couldn't, and if I sat at Liam's table then that would only drive his suspicions further. Instead I opted for quickly going through the line and grabbing an apple and a turkey sandwich. I headed for the doors, food in hand to go back and eat in my dorm.

"LILY!" I heard one of the guys call across the cafeteria. Great, now all eyes were on me.

I pretended I hadn't heard him and walked right on through the doors and across the campus without looking back. I walked in and sat down on my bed taking a bite out of my sandwich. God! I thought girls were all about drama but it was clear that boys had there own drama. How was I ever going to survive? I couldn't avoid for the rest of the year. I would have to face him sometime. Just not right now.

9

I had spent the entire forty-five minute lunch period up in my dorm room, all alone, in complete silence. If you could have seen me, you would have said what a poor, sad, pathetic, girl. I bet she doesn't have any friends. When in fact I do, lots of them! Just not with me right now.

Thankfully I had history next; this was a free ticket away from all of the guys and their questions. I walked by myself across the campus, into the classroom, by myself, and sat down, by myself. Okay maybe I was missing them a little bit. Two seconds later Liam was occupying the empty seat next to me.

"Hey." I said throwing him a small smile

"Hey. Why weren't you at lunch?"

"I ate in my room." I replied dejectedly.

"Why?"

"I didn't want to sit with Will."

"Oh. So that's why you didn't turn around when Oliver called for you."

"Yeah."

"Don't worry, everything will work out. I know it."

"Thanks." I said turning to listen to Mr. Horsh.

Now that I thought about it I could clearly see Liam as a gay guy. At least metro sexual. How had I never noticed this before? He was too nice and comforting to be any normal guy.

I had survived my History class, all thanks to Liam, who explained practically everything to me. This boy was smart too. I had completely forgotten about the other boys, to wrapped up in the lesson and what Liam was saying. So wrapped up that I almost peed my pants when the bell rang.

"Good God!" I said jumping up from my seat.

"Little tense?" Liam asked jokingly.

"Just startled me."

"Well you better get to your next class don't want to be late." He said gathering his books and heading for the door, me behind him.

"Bye!" I called as we parted going in different directions, him to literature, me to chemistry.

I walked into the chemistry room and my mood instantly fell. I had forgotten that every last one of the guys shared this class with me, and to top it all of Will was my lab partner. Someone up there hates me! Maybe it was that goldfish I had when I was seven, two weeks, then down the drain!

I silently walked over and put my books on the table that I shared with Will. He was already there, and seemed to tense up when I approached. I placed my books in between us forming a barrier. I noticed John look at his twin and give him a look, who in turn gave the same look to Cal, who gave it to Dave, then Ian, and lastly Oliver. What the hell?

They were soooooo planning something! Oh well it didn't matter, they couldn't do anything, after this class they had training and I was free to do what I wanted. I did my best to ignore Will and focus on writing down everything that came out of Mr. Gale's mouth. Until he got really, really, really, boring, then I just doodled on the side of my paper.

The bell rang and I jumped up out of my chair and ran for the door, I was the first one out of the room, I made sure of that! Not giving anyone a chance to talk to me or ask questions I rushed back to my dorm and closed the door. I would only be alone for an hour. What about when they came back? I quickly made up my mind and changed into a pair of black track pants and a baby blue tee with my gray jacket.

I slipped out the door and headed outside for some fresh air, hopefully to clear my mind. I could see the obstacle course off in the distance with several figures climbing and crawling on top of and over it. Not gonna go that way! I turned on my heel and headed in the opposite direction towards the way I had first come when I had arrived here.

Walking down the smooth drive to the front entrance I kicked a pebble along with the toe of my shoe. I stopped when I reached the sign. This had been the first thing I had seen on my arrival here. Now I had a good chance to look at it and read the WHOLE thing. 'Wilmington Military Academy for Young Men'

I hoisted myself up onto the top of the stone sign and sat looking away from the school and everything around it. This was the first time I had noticed that the front entrance was covered in trees, almost like a forest.

How I would LOVE to just get up right now and walk out. See what was beyond the entrance. Was I ever going to get to leave? Was I going to live her forever and never even know what was out beyond the borders? I think not.

I hopped down off the sign and started for the trees. I hadn't taken two steps before I heard someone calling my name. Sighing I turned around knowing that my 'expedition' would have to wait for another day.

"LILY!" Dave yelled as he ran up to me. He looked worried.

"What?" I said walking towards him.

"You have to come. Come on!" He grabbed my wrist and started running back towards the school

"What's wrong?" I asked my voice filled with worry as I stumbled after him.

He didn't respond. He just kept running.

"Dave!"

Running.

"DAVE!" I yelled as he pulled me through the doors to the dorm lobby and into the elevator.

As soon as the doors slid open he ran down the hall still holding onto my wrist and thrust open my door. All I could think of was that someone was hurt. Ian, Oliver,...Will. My worry was quickly erased when I was pulled in and saw all the guys sitting in the room, perfectly fine. Nobody was dead, nobody was hurt, at least they weren't yet.

"What the hell is going on?" I asked the group after Dave had let go of my arm and went to stand with the other guys.

"We noticed that you have been avoiding us." Oliver spoke up.

"Are you kidding me? You drug me here to tell me that! I thought one of ya'll were hurt or dead!"

"Dave is a good actor." Jason pointed out.

"Thanks." Dave said.

"Focus." Oliver stated.

"Like I was saying. We noticed that you've been avoiding us."

"No I'm not!" I lied.

"Then why weren't you at breakfast?"

"I wasn't hungry."

"Why did you sit across the room in Pre-Cal?"

"There were only three seats left so I was being nice and let ya'll have them!" I shot at them angrily, getting defensive.

"Why didn't you eat lunch with us?"

"I didn't feel good."

"That's a lie." Ian put in.

"Oh so now you know my medical state?"

"Lily."

"WHAT?" I screamed at them.

Couldn't they see I didn't want to talk to them at the moment? Especially with Will in the room. Take a hint, bad mood + Lily disaster. I had my arms crossed in front of my chest and my right hip was popped out to the side.

This was a clear sign that I was pissed and that you were not supposed to mess with me.

"You've been acting weird ever since I saw you with Liam in the library." Will spoke up. I noticed that his arms like mine were also crossed.

"GOD! Is that what this is all about?" I said throwing my hands in the air in frustration.

They all just looked at me with the same look. Concern and worry. Will seemed to also seem a little jealous but I was too mad to even care. They were concerned and worried for me over LIAM! LIAM! If they only knew! He is the guy that they should be worried the least about. They had a better chance of it snowing in 90-degree weather.

"We don't want to see you get hurt." Will said in a softer tone.

"I'm not going to get hurt, because there is NOTHING going on between me and Liam!"

"Nothing?" Will said raising an eyebrow.

"Nothing. I promise. You can ask him yourself."

"We already did." John interjected.

"You WHAT? So you didn't believe him and decided to interrogate me too?"

"We couldn't be sure."

"Whatever."

"So there's nothing going on with you and Liam?" Will asked yet again.

"No, and if there was it's not any of your business whom I choose to date or not!"

"Sorry." He said casting his eyes to the ground.

Damn guilt! It was like staying mad at an adorable puppy. You just couldn't. No matter how muchI wanted to be mad at Will I just couldn't. The same went for the rest of the guys. It was like one big litter of adorable, mischievous puppies. I swear I was tempted to go over and pet him on the head!

These boys were definitely going to take a toll on my emotions. Angry Lily would most likely show up more often, but disappear just as quickly. I guess what they say is right. Boys can't live with them, can't live without them. I was living proof of that.

10

S aturday, the best day ever. There was no school, no homework, no getting up early, just doing whatever the hell I felt like doing. I loved Saturdays. I had woken up at a reasonable hour, only to notice that all of the boys were already up. They were pulling on various articles of clothing; thank God I hadn't woken up a second earlier.

"What are you guys doing?" I asked climbing out of my bed and pulling down on my pink tank top, which had ridden up as I tossed in my sleep.

"Getting ready." Will said pulling on his left shoe.

"For what?"

"Every Saturday everyone is allowed to leave campus and go into town."

"Really?" I asked excitedly.

"Yeah."

"I am SO coming!" I yelled and dashed for the closet.

I shut the doors and picked out my clothes. I slipped into a pair of jeans and pulled a dark green polo shirt on. I opened the doors to find all the guys waiting for me. I slipped on some tennis shoes and grabbed my jacket and purse.

"So how do we get into town?" I asked walking down the hallway.

"We walk." John stated with a smile.

We made our way across the campus, I noticed that several large groups of boys were heading the same way.

"I see everyone likes getting away."

"Trust me. We take every chance we can to get away." John said raising his eyebrows.

We passed the entrance sign, I was getting out, just like I had wanted. I thought the walk would have been longer, but after five minutes we reached the town. It wasn't a large town, but it seemed that it was a haven for the boys. Of course this became my new haven when I saw all of the shops.

"SHOPPING!" I yelled pulling on Cal's arm and dragging him towards the first store I saw.

"What? No way! We're not going shopping!"

"Why else would we be here?" I scoffed continuing to pull him towards the shop.

"Not to shop." He protested pulling back on my arm and dragging me away.

"CAL!" I whined stretching my free arm out to the shop.

He pulled me back over to the group, which was now laughing.

"I want to go shopping!"

"We don't." Cal stated.

"Come on Cal. Have a heart give the lady what she wants." Will said punching him in the arm.

"FINE!" Dave let out a long sigh and looped his arm through mine. "She can have me."

"I meant the shopping."

"We all know she wants me." He said smirking down at me.

I smiled up at him and leaned in close to his ear.

"You're right Dave. I can't stop thinking about you... DRESSED UP IN MY CLOTHES!" I yelled the last part.

He removed his arm from mine and clamped a hand over my mouth.

"SHHH! That never gets out!"

"It won't get out if we go shopping." I said rocking back and forth on my heels.

"Shopping it is then!" He declared and started for the shop with us following him.

The tiny silver bell connected to the door rang when we entered the shop. It was a cramped shop packed with various items of clothing and accessories. My eyes feel onto a set of eight silver bangle bracelets. I HAD to have them!

I ran over to them and grabbed them from their resting-place. There was really no reason to run. I mean there were no other customers in the store, except for the guys, and I don't think they would have fought me over them. At least I hoped they wouldn't, because I'm pretty sure they would have won...maybe.

I walked up to the register were an old lady was sitting reading a worn paper back book. I sat the bangles on the counter with a small jangle and she looked up. She smiled at me and her eyes all but disappeared in her wrinkles. She rang me up and I paid her. The minute we were out side of the shop I slipped them onto my wrists, four on each arm.

"What did you buy?" Will asked as we walked along the street.

"These." I said holding up my wrists for him to see. They slid down my arm with a light tinkle of sound.

"Nice."

The remainder of the day was spent going in and out of shops. I ended up with two new shirts; a pair of earrings and of course my bangles. Currently we were sitting down at a large table in front of this really cute restaurant and eating lunch. Oh yeah, and I was listening to the boys complain.

"My feet hurt." Jason whined.

"Mine too." His twin put in.

"Suck it up." I retorted.

"We just spent two hours shopping!" Cal cried.

"And in return your little transvestite secret stays a secret."

"How can you stand all of that shopping?" Will asked from beside me as he stole a chip from me.

"Are you serious? Ya'll can run around on an obstacle course for who knows how long, do a million pushups, but you can't take shopping? Pathetic." I said taking my chip back before he ate it.

"Shopping is hard! I don't see how you do it."

"This was a SMALL shopping trip. I've been known to go on a seven-hour spree. Don't test me."

"SMALL! It'll take me a month to get over this traumatizing experience."

"And that is why, boys hate shopping. They can't deal with the emotional stress it brings!"

"Hey! I just noticed something!" Oliver all but yelled.

"What?"

"You have eight bracelets!"

"DUH! Did you miss that when I bought them?"

"No. Eight bracelets, one for each of us!"

"You're right! I'll wear one for each of my boys!" I chirped up.

'There's only seven guys, you're a girl. Remember?" Will said with a laugh.

"No. There's eight. You, Ian, Oliver, Dave, Cal, John, Jason, and Liam." I said pointing to a bracelet with each name.

"Liam?"

"Yeah. Liam is my friend too you know." I said glaring at him.

Will let out a long sigh. I rolled my eyes and stood up from the table and picked up my recently purchased items along with my purse. I headed back in the direction we had came from.

"Where are you going?" Will called out as all of the boys stood up and followed me.

I didn't respond, I just ignored him and kept walking. Why couldn't he just accept that Liam and I were friends?

"Lily!" He called again.

"What?" I asked turning around.

"Wait up!"

I scoffed and turned around. I bumped into someone and almost fell down. I would have if the person had not caught me by my arm. I looked up to find Liam's smiling face looking down at me.

"Hey." He said letting go of my arm.

"Hey. What are you doing here?" I asked.

"Some of the guys and me were taking the opportunity to get away." He said motioning to the group of five guys behind him. I recognized one of the guys to be Quinton. The one who had bluntly asked to go out with me.

"Oh." I said feeling stupid. Of course that's why everyone was here.

"I see you've been shopping. How did you get your group of bodyguards to agree to that?" He said jerking his head in the direction of the group of guys fast approaching with an agitated Will leading the pack.

"AH! That's my secret." I said winking at him.

"Liam." Will said in a cold tone as he stepped up beside me.

"Will." He responded in the same tone.

I looked back and forth between the guys who were what looked like having a glaring contest. Boys could be so immature.

"Well we better be going." I said breaking the silence. "Bye Liam!" I called as I grabbed Will's hand and began to drag him back in the direction of the school.

"What was that about?" I asked as we made our way back onto the campus.

"I told you I don't like the guy." Will said looking down at me.

"Whatever." I said rolling my eyes.

We were headed towards our dorm building when we passed the offices and my Uncle Eric stuck his head out of the door.

"Lily. Can I have a word with you please?" He asked.

"Um.. Yeah." I said as I started towards him. Only then did I notice that I was still holding onto Will's hand. Great.

I detached my hand from Will's and walked into the small office. He motioned for me to sit in the small chair in front of his desk that he was sitting behind. I felt like a little kid that had just been discovered with her hand in the cookie jar and was being scolded for it.

"You wanted to talk to me?" I said trying to make this go as fast as possible.

"Yes. I just wanted to know how you were adjusting."

Whew! I thought he was going to bring up Will!

"Fine." I responded as I relaxed.

"Are you sure? Is there anything you need?"

"Nope."

"What about your roommates?" He said.

Nevermind! There was the million-dollar question!

"Good. There all really nice." I said trying to choose my words carefully.

"No trouble?"

"None."

"Well, that's good to hear." He said seeming to loosen up.

"Is that all you wanted?" I asked eager to get out and go back to my dorm.

"Yes. You can go."

"Thanks. Bye Uncle Eric" I called heading for the door.

"Lily." He said before I could leave.

"Yeah?" I asked turning my hand still on the doorknob.

"If you need anything, or if you want to talk just come find me." He said smiling.

"I will." I replied with a smile of my own.

I walked out and closed the door behind me. I headed back towards my dorm. Well that was a hallmark moment. It felt like I was in some kind of movie. You know the kind where the girl that looses her parents confides in her new guardian. Yeah I guess I left that whole confiding part out.

"Hey. What did General McKain want?" Will asked the second I stepped over the threshold.

"Oh. He Just wanted to know how I was adjusting." I said flopping on my bed.

"Oh."

An awkward silence filled the room. It seemed like the three boys wanted to ask me something more but had decided against it. I sat up and crossed my legs in front of me.

"What?" I asked looking as each of them.

"Nothing." They all replied a little too quickly.

"Nothing my butt, tell me." I demanded.

"It's just that General McKain doesn't seem like the caring type that would bother to ask how you were doing. What did he really want?" Will piped up from beside me.

"What? My uncle is a very nice man!" I protested.

Oops.

I swear each of their mouths fell open! How the hell did I let that slip out of my mouth? Great, this was just perfect! I did NOT want that piece of information to get around. Everyone would be too scared to even look at me, let alone talk to me!

"He's your uncle?" Oliver all but choked on his words.

"Yeah."

"So that's how you got in."

"Yeah."

"I knew they wouldn't let a girl come here for any normal reason."

"Really, it's not that big of a deal." I said standing up.

"Sure it is! It's huge! We're rooming with our drill sergeants niece!" Ian said in a panicked voice.

"Calm down. He's not gonna kill ya or anything." I said rolling my eyes. "And I don't want any of ya'll to get all weird and not talk to me or anything."

"Okay." Will said in a calm voice. He actually didn't seem to care.

"Really?" I asked turning towards him.

"Yeah. It's fine. Now come on. I'm hungry, I want dinner."

"Me too."

"Same here."

Boys. Food was always the number one thing on their priority list.

"Fine." I agreed following them out the door.

"So your uncle is General McKain?" John asked from across the table.

We were all seated at our usual table. The guys stuffing their faces and I was trying not to puke when they talked with their mouths full of food.

"Yep." I said picking up my burger and taking a bite out of it.

It had taken forever to get Dave to stop asking me if he was going to die. After a million no's, I finally told him that if he didn't stop asking he wouldn't have to worry about it because I would kill him myself. That shut him up.

We were walking out of the cafeteria when I saw Cal stop in front of the bulletin board and then let out a groan.

"What?" I asked him.

"That." He said pointing to a piece of yellow paper tacked to the board.

I quickly read what had been typed on the paper and a feeling of dread washed over me. What was I going to do? This couldn't be happening! Why here, why now? How was I going to lie my way out of this one?

"I hate parents day!" Cal stated.

"What is it?" I choked out

"It's a day were all of the parents come and visit. It's mainly just a day for the teachers to show off." Will said shrugging his shoulders" It's not that bad. All of the parents usually bring presents and stuff."

Parents day. How was I going to get around this mess? When my parents don't show up, everyone is going to start asking questions, especially Will. I still wasn't ready to tell anyone yet. From the looks of it I had one week to figure out what I was going to do. Right now I was completely and totally screwed.

A/N: Who's your favorite guy so far?

Thank you for reading! :)

11

The remainder of the weekend had passed quicker than I had liked. It was Monday, that meant it was back to school. I could tell that today was not going to be a good day. Why? Well, first of all the minute I woke up I was met with the problem of parents day only being six days away. Secondly, my hair looked like crap. Thirdly, I poked myself in the eye with my mascara wand. Today was definitely not going to be a good day.

"Hey Lily." Cal said as I sat down at the table with my two pieces of toast and scrambled eggs.

"Eh." I grunted in return.

"Looks like someone has a case of the Monday's!" John threw in.

He had no idea how right he was. Monday is the worst day of the week. I think God created Monday just to piss people off, he did a hell of a job if that was his intention. I picked at my eggs and only ate one piece of toast, before the bell rang to go to first period. I lazily followed the guys to my first class praying for this day to end.

Why when you pray for something to end quickly it seems to drag on forever? To start off I had a pop quiz in Pre-Cal, which I barely passed.

Then I was forced to continue to participate in a horrible sport I call basketball, followed by a sleep-induced lecture in history. Yeah today pretty much sucked.

I said my good byes to the guys as they hurried off towards their training. I entered my dorm room and promptly collapsed onto my bed. My eyes closed, as I lay sprawled across the surface of the bed. I quickly drifted off into sleep and into my hellish nightmare.

I stared out at the empty street in front of me. I could barley make out an approaching figure in the heavy fog. As the object drew closer I could make out the shape of a car and see the thin beams of light emitted from the headlights. I glanced in the other direction and saw another car approaching much faster than the previous one.

It increased in speed with every passing second. My eyes fell onto the other vehicle, which was now gliding past me in a state that seemed to be slow motion. The other car was there in a matter of seconds.

The harsh sound of crunching metal filled my ears and shards of broken, jagged, glass flew in every direction. The remains of the two cars sat lifeless on the quiet street. I walked over to the car that had been hit. I stooped down to look through the broken window; these people were probably hurt and needed help.

A woman with dirty blonde hair matted with blood was sitting in the passenger seat, next to a man with dark brown hair. Blood was dripping down his face from a deep gash in his head. Their lifeless fingers enter twined in one last loving embrace. My parents.

I sat up quickly the images disappearing from behind my eyelids, but forever imprinted in my memory. I touched my face and found tears. I glanced at the clock and saw that the guys would be back soon. I quickly wiped away all evidence of my tears away and got up.

Not wanting to be here when they returned I hurried out the door and made my way outside. In the distance I could see groups of guys walking towards their dorms. I took off at a brisk pace to the library. I needed to be somewhere quiet, and that was about the only place around here that guaranteed it.

I pushed open the heavy glass doors and was greeted with blissful silence. There were a few younger boys sitting together at one table studying; they didn't bother to look up when the door closed. I made my way over into a deserted corner and flopped down into a large, black, leather, armchair. I closed my eyes and rested my head against the back of the chair lost in thought.

"Lily?"

I opened my eyes to find a boy with light brown hair and caramel colored eyes staring down at me. Quinton.

"Yeah?" I replied sitting up straighter.

"Were you just sleeping?"

"No, just thinking. I needed some alone time." I said hoping he would take the hint and go away.

He sat down in the chair next to mine, oblivious to the gigantic hint I threw his way.

"I'm surprised to see you buy yourself."

'I'm not by myself anymore.' I thought.

"All of the guys were at training." I replied shortly.

"I'm glad that I found you alone. I wanted to ask you something."

Not again! This boy was going to ask me out again! I had already turned him down once after he asked me after only have known me for three seconds! Couldn't he take a hint and just go away? Did he enjoy rejection this much?

"I was wondering if- -"

"Lily!" He was cut off by an approaching form. Liam! My savior.

"Hey Liam!" I called jumping out of my chair.

"Quinton." He said nodding to the frustrated boy that had stood up as well.

"Hey." He replied in a gruff voice.

"I hope you don't mind but I need to borrow Lily here for awhile. I'll see you back at the room." He called over his shoulder as he grasped his wrist and pulled me towards the exit.

Once outside he let go of my wrist and we continued to walk across the campus.

"Thanks."

"No problem. I could tell by the look on your face that you would have done anything to get away."

"You know me too well." I said with a laugh.

"Don't be surprised if you get a lot more guys coming up and asking you out though."

"Why?" I asked out of curiosity.

He stopped walking and turned to face me as I stopped beside him. He gave me a disbelieving look and shook his head.

"For one you're the only girl here, two, you're absolutely gorgeous, and three, most of these guys around here are pretty damn horny."

"Okay I agree with the first and third ones but I'm not that pretty."

"Of course you are! Do you not own a mirror?"

"Yes I own a mirror."

"Do you ever look in it?"

"Yes, Liam." I said sighing.

"Then you should know that you are the most beautiful girl I have ever seen!"

I blushed and looked away. That's when I saw Will standing but only three feet away. By the look on his face he had caught the end of or conversation, thanks to Liam's yelling protest. Before I could get a word out he turned and walked away, back towards the dorm room.

GREAT! How did he always appear at such horrible times? Every time I was with Liam he seemed to show up and assume the worst. Turning to Liam I gave him a small sigh.

"Guess I better go do some damage control."

"Yeah. Good luck!" He said with a smile and a wave as he turned and walked away.

I arrived back at the room to find all three guys spread out on each of their beds. They seemed to be in deep conversation about something. Probably me.

"Will." I said as I shut the door.

He turned to look at me and the turned back around and continued his conversation as though I wasn't standing five feet away from him! Oh he was going to get it!

"Will!" I said storming over to his bedside.

Once again he turned to look at me. This time I was ready. Just as he was about to turn around, I caught the sleeve of his shirt and forced him to face me yet again. Oliver and Ian exchanged glances but remained seated.

"Do you need something?" He asked looking down at his sleeve clutched in my fist.

"Why are you mad at me?"

"Why did you lie to me?" He shot back.

"What are you talking about?" I cried releasing my grip on his shirt.

"You said there was nothing going on between you and Liam."

"There's not!" I yelled throwing my hands up in the air.

"Not what I got out of it! 'You're the most beautiful girl I have ever seen.'" He said quoting Liam.

"So now you're spying on me!"

"I just happened to walk by and heard you all."

"You know what, I don't have to talk about this!" I said stomping over and lying on my bed facing away from him.

"So you are going out with him."

"NO!" I yelled turning over. "Actually you should be thanking him!"

"For what?"

"He came in right when Quinton was about to ask me out... AGAIN!"

"Quinton asked you out? What did you say?"

"He didn't get a chance to ask. Liam came in and said he needed me."

"Then he asked you out?"

"Who?"

"Liam."

"NO! Liam has NEVER asked me out, kissed me, or anything!"

GOD! How many times was I going to have to explain that to this boy? It would be SO much easier if only he knew Liam was gay, but there was NO way I was going to let his secret slip. I promised him, and I intended to keep that promise.

"So I'm supposed to believe you when you say that nothing's going on between you two?"

"YES!" I yelled jumping up from my bed. "That's what friends do! They trust each other!"

"How can I trust you when you lied to me; to all of us?"

"I DIDN'T LIE TO ANY OF YOU!"

"How do I know that you aren't lying right now?" He asked his temper rising along with mine.

"You know what? I don't have to stand here and listen to you accuse me of things I didn't do!" I yelled as I stomped towards the door, grabbing my purse along the way.

"Where are you going?" Will asked getting off of his bed.

"It doesn't concern you!" I shot back slamming the door in his face.

I quickly made my way to the elevator and pressed the button. I heard the door close again and approaching footsteps. I pressed the elevator button again, willing it to come faster. Unfortunately luck was not on my side.

Will appeared by my side seconds before the elevator doors slid open. Great. I walked in without even sparing him a glance; well in this case it would be more of a glare. He walked in and leaned against the opposite wall.

The doors slid shut and the elevator started to descend. We were about to pass the second floor when Will leaned over and pressed the emergency stop button. The elevator jerked to a stop, causing me to stumble. I caught myself with my outstretched hand against the wall.

"What the hell is wrong with you?" I yelled at him, reaching for the button.

He blocked my way by moving in front of the buttons and crossing his arms over his chest. I looked at him like he was crazy and he returned the same look. I crossed my arms over my chest mirroring him and leaned against the wall. If he thought I was going to talk to him just because he trapped me in an elevator he had another thing coming to him.

"Lily."

I looked in the other direction pretending I hadn't heard him.

"Lily."

LALALA! I CAN'T HEAR YOU!

"Stop being childish." He said with a scoff.

"I'm being childish! You're the one who trapped me in an elevator!"

"Got you to talk." He said a smile creeping onto his lips.

Damn.

"So what? What do you want?"

"I want you to tell me the truth."

"I am telling the truth! Why won't you believe me?" I said looking him straight in the eye.

"It's kind of hard to believe someone when they say one thing and then you see them doing the exact opposite."

"You just walk into conversations and pick up on a couple of words and then jump to conclusions."

"I'm not sure if I even want to hear the rest of those conversations." He said looking pointedly at me.

"I'm not a whore."

"I didn't say you were." He said uncrossing his arms. His eyes softening.

"You implied it."

"I didn't mean to."

"Why do you even care about Liam and I so much?"

"I told you. I don't want to see you get hurt." He said looking at the ground.

"That's not it. There has to be more to it than that."

His chocolate brown eyes shot up from the ground and met mine. There was something in them. I couldn't tell what it was. I didn't need to know what his eyes were trying to tell me, he told me himself.

"I don't want to see you with him because..."

"What?"

"I like you. More than just a friend."

WOAH! Back up! Is he serious! This hot GQ model likes me! ME! As in plain southern girl me? WOW! I mean... actually I don't know what I mean! I'm dumb struck at the moment.

"Now you know." He said reaching for the button to start the elevator again.

I reached out and grabbed his hand to stop him.

"Why?" I asked looking up at him; our hands still clasped together.

"Why what?"

"Why me? Why do you like me?"

"Why wouldn't I? You're beautiful, smart, funny, caring, and to top it all off you put up with all of us every day." He said with a smile.

I let my own smile spread across my face.

"I like you too." I confessed biting my bottom lip.

"You do?" He asked looking surprised.

"Yeah."

"You don't know how much better you just made me feel." He said pulling on my hand to bring me into a tight hug.

"So what does this mean?" I asked after he was finished with crushing me.

"I think it means that we're in a relationship. That is if you want to." He said quickly.

"No. I want to."

"Good." He said leaning down and pressing his lips gently against my own.

He pulled away and smiled. He reached behind him and pressed the button. The elevator jerked back to life and started to descend again. This time I didn't stumble because Will was there to hold onto me. I guess Mondays aren't so bad after all.

12

"I still can't believe it." Jason said looking back and forth between Will and I, the next morning at breakfast.

"I know. One girl comes here and Will gets her. Can't they send some more for the rest of us?" John added.

"Or we could just share." Jason stated looking hopefully at Will.

"I'm not sharing. She's mine." Will stated firmly holding my hand up for all to see.

"Come on Will. Didn't they teach you to share when you were little?" I said messing with him.

"I never was any good at it." He said smiling at me.

He kissed me lightly, gaining a groan from all the other guys around the table. I looked at them and stuck my tongue out.

"If we have to deal with this everyday, then I'm going to end up killing one of you two." Dave said.

"You? Oliver and I have to live with the them!"

"Hey!" I yelled smacking him in the arm.

"Attention students!" A crackling voice called over the intercom. "Don't forget that Parent's Day will be here soon. We want to remind everyone to be on their best behaviors. Also, will Ms. Lily Daniels, please report to General McKain's office now. Thank you."

THUMP, THUMP, THUMP!

I looked over and saw Cal repeatedly banging his head against the table. I felt like doing the exact same thing. Instead I got up from my seat, waved good-bye to all of the boys and strode off to my Uncle's office.

I knocked on the wooden door and stuck my head in.

"You wanted to see me?" I asked.

"Oh. Hello, Lily. Come in." My Uncle said with a warm smile from behind his desk.

I plopped down in the chair that was seated across from his desk and crossed my legs.

"As I'm sure you're aware that Parent's Day is this Friday."

"Yes."

"I know it will be hard on you, with all the other parents being here, and I was wondering if you would like to have the day off, to go off campus and enjoy the day?"

Here it was my perfect opportunity. This was exactly what I had needed. However it just didn't feel right. It felt like a cop-out, like I was running away. Hadn't that been what I was doing all along though? Maybe it was time to stop running and face it. My parents were dead, they were not coming back, and no one would ever replace them.

"It's okay. I think I can handle it."

"Are you sure?" He asked sounding surprised.

"Yeah."

"Well, if that's how you feel, I guess I can't force you."

"Is that all you needed to talk to be about?" I asked wanting to get out and away from the awkwardness.

"Yes. Here take this note, so you won't be marked late for class." He said passing me a small piece of crisp white paper that had been folded neatly.

"Thanks." I called over my shoulder as I closed the door.

I made my way to my first class, the entire time thinking about what I had just done. Was I really ready to tell someone? Would I ever be ready to tell someone? Whether I was or not, eventually they would find out. The question I had to ask myself was did I want them to find out from me or from some other source?

I pushed open the door to the classroom and slipped into my seat beside Oliver. He glanced at me and gave me a friendly smile, before returning to the assignment we had been given.

I trudged down the hallway, my mood dampened. Math always does that to me. It's like it just wants to make me miserable and see me unhappy. Yeah math sucks.

"Not happy to see me?" A deep voice called out.

I looked up and saw Will leaning against the wall outside of our math class.

"Not when you're standing by that room."

"What?"

"Nothing."

He sauntered forward and kissed my forehead.

"You're always happy to see me and you know it."

"Of course." I replied shuffling into the dungeon. Excuse me math class.

"Fucking torture." I said stepping out of the class with a boat load of homework in my arms.

"I didn't think it was that bad." Will said from beside me.

"Yeah because you're his favorite."

"Am not!"

"Oh please! 'Wonderful work Will! Nice job Will! Yes Will!'" I said lowering my voice trying to impersonate our math teacher.

"So I'm good at math."

"Obviously." I said glancing at his arms to see that he had already finished his homework, stupid math genius.

"Stupid math genius." I muttered under my breath.

"How can I be stupid, if I am a genius?"

"Exactly."

"What?"

"Yep."

"What are you talking about?"

"Totally."

"You make no sense, but I like you anyway." He said wrapping an arms around my waist as we entered the gym.

"I know!" I smiled happily up at him.

My smile faded as I saw a rack of basketballs waiting to humiliate. Would the torture never end?

"I hate basketball." I stated sitting down at the lunch table.

All of the guys looked up at me. Cal had ketchup smeared on his right cheek. I reached over and wiped it off with a napkin. He squirmed around in his seat trying to evade me.

"Stop!" He whined.

"Hold still. You have ketchup on your face."

"You're not my mother!"

"Fine. Go around with ketchup smeared all over your face for the rest of the day I don't care." I said crossing my arms and looking away.

He went back to eating his lunch. I glanced at him out of the corner of my eye. I quickly grabbed the napkin and pounced on him. I managed to remove the smudge from his face and sat back happily. The rest of the guys laughed at Cal as he sat pouting.

"That's better!" I quipped sitting back and picking up my sandwich.

"You know you're dating a psycho right?" Cal said looking at Will.

"Yeah."

"Hey!" I yelled punching him on the arm.

"But she's my psycho."

"HA!" I said sticking my tongue out at Cal.

The bell rang signaling the end of lunch and we all stood up.

"Ready to go to history?" Liam asked coming up behind me.

"Yep!" I replied.

I turned around and gave Will a short hug and a kiss.

"Just friends." I whispered to him before waving and walking off with Liam.

"So I see you got your prince." Liam said as we walked out of the cafeteria.

"I guess I did."

"So are your parents flying in for parent's day?" He asked casually.

My stomach twisted in a knot, and I could feel the tears sting the back of my eyes. I held them back and took a deep breath.

"No. They can't make it."

"Really? Mine either."

"You're parents aren't coming?"

"No, they have more important things to do than to come see their youngest son." He said with a tinge of anger in his voice.

I was going to ask him about it but the bell rang as we stepped through the doorway and class started.

I walked into chemistry and took my seat next to Will.

"How was history with Liam?" He asked.

"Fine, and I told you, we're just friends."

"Okay." He said seeming to relax.

"I don't know why you don't like him." I said pulling out my text book.

"I just never have."

"Why?"

"I just don't like him."

"Well there has to be a reason." I pushed.

"No. We just never liked each other. Some people just don't click."

"That's-"

"Ms. Daniels. Please stop talking." Mr. Gale called out from the front of the room.

"Sorry." I muttered, turning my attention back to my book.

After about fifteen minutes of listening to Mr. Gale drone on about electron configurations, I blocked him out and started singing in my head. I had a very nice song running through my head when Will shook me out of it.

"You ruined my song!" I exclaimed.

"What?" He asked looking confused.

"Nevermind. What do you want?"

"Class is over." He said motioning towards the boy spilling out of the room and heading off to training.

"Guess I blanked out." I said smiling sheepishly. "Did I miss anything important?"

"No. He got off topic and started talking about how he used to play ice hockey." He said as we proceeded to exit the classroom.

"I guess I'll see you after training." He said placing a quick kiss on my lips.

"Okay. I'll see you later." I waved goodbye as he jogged down the hall to catch up with the rest of the guys.

I turned and started back to my dorm room. I was halfway across the quad when I had a brilliant idea. I sprinted back to our dorm room and threw my stuff down on my bed. I rushed to the closet and changed into a pair of jeans and a long sleeve shirt.

I took off towards the training field with a smile on my face. I stopped short of the obstacle course and looked around. I spotted Will climbing over a wall and heading towards me obliviously.

I ducked under the net crawl and lay on the ground. I only had to wait a minute before the net began to shake with the weight of Will crawling on top of it. I waited until he was practically on top of me.

"WILL!" I screamed.

He jumped back in surprise and his feet fell through the holes in the net. He looked around confused at who had screamed at him. A stream of giggles poured out from my mouth before I could stop them. He looked down and saw me lying on the ground grinning up at him.

"What are you doing?" He whispered.

"Having fun! Now go more people are coming and don't tell anyone!" I ordered as I saw Cal's head peak over the top of the net.

"Stop stalling Will!" He called from the top of the net.

Will quickly glanced down at me with a smile and continued on. Cal rolled down the net and proceeded to crawl in my direction. His hand landed in the perfect spot. My hand shot up through the net of ropes and grabbed his arm. He let out a high pitched scream and fell backwards. This was a better reaction than Will's. He glared down at me about to say something when another boy yelled at him to move. He took off as I lie there awaiting my next victim.

I crawled out from under the net after all of the boys had finished the obstacle course and were preparing to leave. I bent down to brush the dirt off of my clothes. I straightened up to find all of my boys looking at me.

"Hi!" I greeted them bubbly.

"Why where you under there?" John asked.

"Under where?" I asked playing dumb.

"The net crawl, scaring the shit out of us!"

"Ooh! That! I got bored." I stated simply before walking off.

I felt a pair of arms wrap around my waist before being hoisted into the air. The next thing I know, I was air-born, flying, well more like falling, onto the net. Will jumped up onto the net and straddled me.

"Get off!" I whined trying to push him off.

"Say you're sorry."

"For what?"

"For scaring the shit out of us. Especially Cal. Bye the way," He said turning his head towards Cal. "Nice girlie scream."

"Shut up!"

"So are you going to apologize?"

"Nope."

"Fine" He said placing his hands on my sides.

"You wouldn't."

"Are you sorry?"

"No."

"Then I would."

I erupted in fits of laughter and giggles as Will assaulted my tummy with his fingers. I squirmed around underneath him, which didn't make the situation any better.

"Mr. Rollens what do you think you are doing?" A deep voice called not but three feet away.

The tickling abruptly stopped and I turned my head to the side to find my uncle, with his arms crossed in front of him and a scowl on his face. Will quickly got off of me and helped me off of the net.

"Uncle Eric we were just- -"

"No excuses Ms. Daniels, and do not address me informally."

My mouth practically fell open. This wasn't the uncle I remembered from when I was little, this wasn't even the same man from a couple of hours ago.

"I want to see you and Mr. Rollens in my office now." He said turning on his heel and allowing Will and I to walk in front of him with our heads down.

13

"I can explain!" I blurted out the second my butt hit the seat.

"Please do. I would love to hear the explanation of why I found Mr. Rollens here on top of my niece." He said from behind his desk shooting a glare at Will.

"Uh..I..Well you see.. we-"

"Sir." Will paused waiting for permission to continue. My Uncle gave a curt nod signaling him to continue.

I held my breath not knowing what he was going to say. God I hope it's not something stupid! Please don't be stupid Will, please. Make up a really good excuse! Anything, like you tripped and fell or something, I don't know! ANYTHING! My mental panic attack ended when Will's voice broke through my thoughts.

"Lily and I are a couple."

Okay! Maybe that will work.

"When did this happen?" My Uncle asked looking towards me for an answer.

"Monday." I answered quietly.

"Well be that as it may, that does not explain why you were down at the obstacle course in the first place."

"I was bored." I offered in my defense.

"That does not give you an excuse to interrupt my lesson."

"Sorry."

"Lily you need to pack your things."

Oh my God! Was he kicking me out? Where the hell was I supposed to go! I would have to go to foster care! This cannot be happening; he's my legal guardian he can't just throw me out!

"What? Why?" I asked afraid of what his answer was going to be.

"I am reassigning you to a new dorm room. I can't have my niece living with her boyfriend it is out of the question. You need to have all of your things packed and placed in the hallway by tomorrow morning. I will have someone bring them to your new room during your classes. You may go now."

I couldn't believe my ears! I did not want to move rooms! I was perfectly fine where I was. What if my new roommates turned out to be perverted freaks! I could not deal with that.

"Thank you sir." Will said standing up and leading me out of the room.

We made our way across the quad heading for our dorm.

"Can you believe him?" I asked angrily.

"Lily."

"Seriously! It wasn't that big of a deal! He's acting liked I killed someone!"

"Lily."

"This is so not fair!"

"LILY!"

"What?" I asked turning to face him annoyed that he had interrupted my rant.

"I think he has a point."

"What?"

"I can understand. I know if I was in his position, I wouldn't want my only niece living with her boyfriend."

"But-"

"It could have been a lot worse."

"How?"

"One or both of us could have got expelled."

"Could not."

"Well maybe not but I think we got off pretty easy. Don't get me wrong I don't like the idea of you living with other guys, but there's nothing we can do about it. Come on I'll help you pack." He said stepping off the elevator and into the room.

"You're alive!" Oliver cried when we stepped through the doorway.

"Hardly."

"What?"

"I have to change rooms." I said crossly pulling my suitcases from the closet.

"What!" Ian yelled jumping up from his bed.

"Yeah. I know it sucks, and with my luck I'll probably be moved into a room with a bunch of pervs."

"HEY! We weren't pervs."

"Yeah, but I don't have that good of luck to escape it twice."

"We'll smash any guys face that tries anything." Oliver chimed in.

"Thanks. Hope you all like your new roommate."

"We probably not going to get one."

"Why not?"

"You're most likely moving to a room with an open slot. They don't like to move to many people."

"So I'm a special case, great."

I finished packing all of my things with the help of the guys and crawled into bed, for my last night in my room. Life did not like me right now.

I pulled my suitcases out into the hallway the next morning and proceeded down to breakfast with the guys in tow. I didn't eat much; I had lost my appetite. I survived my first three classes of the morning and headed off towards lunch. I had just sat down at our table when the intercom crackled to life.

"Lily Daniels please report to Sgt. McKain's office."

"Ugh!" I pushed away from the table and stood up walking out of the cafeteria with best wishes from the guys.

I made my way across the quad and knocked on his office door.

"Come in."

I pushed the door open and sat down in one of the seats.

"You wanted to see me?"

"Yes. Here is your new room number and key." He said extending his hand and handing me a small key with then number 221 printed on it."

"Is that all?" I asked getting up and heading for the door not waiting or caring for his response.

"Lily." He called.

I stopped a foot from the door and turned around to face him.

"I expected better from you."

What did he say? My ears must have been blocked. Unfortunately they weren't. I opened my mouth, angry words resting on the tip of my tongue ready to retort, but I decided against it. I turned on my heel, my hair flying behind me and threw the door open, slamming it behind me.

I stormed across the quad back in the direction of the cafeteria. How could he say that? He had basically called me a slut. I had always been the good girl! I never smoked, never did drugs, never drank alcohol, never murdered someone! He was acting as if he had caught me having sex!

"I expected better from you!" I spat during chemistry class. "Can you believe him!"

None of the boys responded. They had never seen this side of me. Sure I had gotten angry with them, but nothing ever like this. This was beyond angry, this was absolutely infuriating.

The bell rang and I gathered up my books and headed for the door.

"Hey." Will called walking up beside me and giving me a quick kiss. "Try not to kill your new roommates."

"I'll try, but if there are dead bodies in the hallway don't blame me."

He gave a short laugh before kissing me again.

"I have to go now. Play nice." He said before walking off in the other direction.

I turned and walked in the opposite direction, heading towards my new dorm. I stepped into the elevator and stopped before I pushed the third button. O moved my finger down and sadly pressed the second button.

I stepped out and headed down the hallway in search of my new room. I stopped in front of the door with the number 221 hanging on it and looked down at my key confirming that it was in fact the right room. I unlocked the door and stepped in. It was an identical copy of my old room.

Three of the beds were neatly made while the second one was sloppily unmade. I made my way over to the vacant bed with my suitcases place next to it, and plopped down. My three roommates were off at training with the rest of the boys. I almost got up to go down to the obstacle course but then remembered the last incident and thought better of it.

Instead I dragged my suitcases over to the closet and started to unpack. I had just finished folding and putting away my last pair of jeans in my drawer when I heard the door open. Guess it's time to meet the perverted freaks.

I walked towards the door and almost peed myself with happiness.

"LIAM!" I yelled running up to the sweaty, surprised figure that stood in the doorway. I threw my arms around him and squeezed.

"Lily? What are you doing here?" He asked looking down at me.

"This is my new room! Thank God you're here! I was so worried that I was going to be living with a bunch of perverted freaks and not this makes it so much better!" I rambled on in my relief.

"You're out new roommate?" I heard a voice ask from behind Liam.

I poked my head around Liam's frame and my spirits fell. Standing behind Liam was a very happy, Quinton. He had a smile plastered on his face a mile wide and he seemed like HE was about to pee himself with happiness.

"Um, Yeah. I am."

"This is great!" He said walking into the room and sitting down on the sloppy bed.

Figures he would be the pig.

"Oi! You're in my way." An unfamiliar voice called not far away.

"Sorry." Liam said moving to the side to reveal a tall boy with copper colored hair and hazel eyes. He looked down surprised to see me.

"Hi. I'm Lily."

"Hunter." He said holding out his hand for me to shake. His eyes traveled down and rested on my chest.

Okay so I got stuck with two perverted freaks; at least I have Liam.

"I'm going down to dinner." I said pulling my hand out of his grasp and side stepping him.

"Okay. See you later." Liam called after me.

"Bye."

"YES!" I heard the sound of slapping hands as I shut the door. No doubt it had been Quinton and Hunter.

I walked into the cafeteria and saw that all seven guys were already seated and tearing into their food. I got in line and got my own dinner and walked over, sitting down next to Will.

"So who's your new roommates?" Will asked turning to me along with everyone else.

"There's one guy named Hunter."

At the sound of his name a few of the guys snickered.

"What?"

"Good luck with him."

"Why?" I asked worried.

"He's a little on the stupid side."

"Oh."

"Who else?"

"Quinton."

No one said anything about him.

"And."

"Liam." I said nervous about what Will would say.

"Liam."

"Yeah."

"Well that's just great." Will said crossing his arms. "That's exactly what I need! The player of the year rooming with my girlfriend."

"Calm down Will. Remember just friends."

"Fine."

"So, do we get to smash any other their faces yet?" John asked hopefully.

"No, John. Not yet." I added in thinking about Hunter.

"It's going to be weird without you in the room from now on." Will said.

"Yeah quiet." Oliver threw in.

"Shut up!"

"He's right! We here you across the hall." Cal said.

"Liars." I said crossing my arms.

"How could you accuse us of such a thing!" Dave said placing a hand over his heart.

"I'm leaving! I don't converse with liars." I said standing up only to be pulled back down by Will.

He wrapped his arms around me and held me firmly in his lap as I wriggled around trying to get free. I finally gave up with a huff and sat still. Will was still laughing along with everyone else.

"It's not funny." I pouted.

"Yes it is." Will said leaning in and giving me a kiss.

It started off as just a small peck but it soon escalated.

"Stop it! You're making me go blind!" John called out covering his eyes.

I pulled away blushing and slipped off of Will's lap. I'm going to go back to my room. I said leaning down and giving Will one last kiss.

"Don't forget if you need anything, I'm not that far away, and if anyone does anything just come get us. Okay?"

"I know. Don't worry about me, I'll be fine." I said waving as I walked out of the cafeteria.

I had a small smile on my face as I made my way back to my new dorm. Maybe life didn't suck so much. I walked into the front lobby of the dorm building and into the elevator. I pushed the second button and looked down at the floor.

A yellow piece of paper caught my eye. I picked it up and my heart dropped. Bold, black letters sprawled across the top. PARENT'S DAY! It was fast approaching. I only had a couple of days left.

The elevator dinged and the doors slid open. I walked out the paper still clutched in my hand, and walked into my room. Hunter was sitting at a desk doing homework, as was Quinton, and Liam was lying on his bed. I threw the crumpled flyer into the trash can and then walked into the closet and changed into a pair of pajamas and hopped into my bed.

I was wrong. Life sucked. Life wasn't fair, life hated me. My parents were gone from my life, and there was nothing that was going to change that. No matter how many wishes I made, prayers I said, or tears I cried. Life sucked. Plain and simple.

14

Now I know why everyone out in the whole world had a wonderful dream before. You know the one where it's better than any dream you've ever had, and it just makes you smile for the rest of the day, and you can't wait to get back to sleep and hopefully have that same dream. Well, if you haven't then I pity you.

Also I know that if you have ever been woken up from such a wonderful dream, before it was over and you were ready to wake up, you're not very happy with what woke you up. Be it an alarm clock, a noisy neighbor, or an annoying roommate. I'll give you one guess which one woke me up.

I swatted the hand that was shaking me rather roughly, and tried to focus on returning back to my dream. However the owner of said hand would not give up. I sat straight up in my bed, picked up my pillow and tossed it at that annoying person. Falling back down onto my bed I discovered that I could no longer sleep seeing as I did not possess a pillow.

I groaned dragging myself out of bed. My eyes cracked open and I saw a smiling Hunter standing over my bed, pillow in hand. I glared at him ran a hand through my mess of hair.

"Good morning to you too." He said happily as I scooted over to the closet.

Perfect, not only was he a perverted freak, but he was also a morning person. I was beginning to dislike Hunter more and more.

I closed the closet doors and slipped my uniform on. I stepped out fully dressed and grabbed my brush, pulling it through my hair and putting it up in a messy bun.

"You ready to go down to breakfast?" Liam asked from behind me.

"Yeah." I replied still sleepy and my mind still on my dream.

We walked out into the hallway and started for the cafeteria. Hunter and Quinton walked ahead of us, quietly chatting, every once in a while throwing a glance back at me over their shoulders.

I had to admit it felt weird walking down for breakfast without my usual group of friends. I always walked in with a pack of guys around me and now I only had three, and I didn't even really count two of them.

We walked into the cafeteria and I got my eggs and orange juice from the line. I turned and started for my regular table when I noticed no one was seated there yet. I guess I was in shock at seeing a clean table, without guys cramming food down their throats.

"Do you want to sit with us? At least until your bodyguards come in?" Liam asked coming up behind me.

I smiled at him and followed him over to his table, which at this point consisted of Quinton Hunter, and two guys I didn't recognize. Quinton and Hunter didn't look as shocked as the other two when I sat down next to Liam.

"Did you sleep okay?" Liam asked before taking a bite of his biscuit.

"Actually, yeah I did." I said smiling at the memory of my dream.

"Good. I wasn't sure if you would be comfortable, it being your first night and all."

"Nope, the boogie man didn't get me." I said putting a forkful of eggs into my mouth.

"Glad to know he's finally gone."

"Guess I scared him away."

My gaze shifted to the other guys seated at the table. They all stared on in silent awe. As if they were amazed that Liam and I could have a conversation. I gave them a weird look before returning my gaze to Liam. Instead it fell on the door behind him.

All seven guys walked in looking tired and headed for the food line.

"I guess I better go, before Will sees me and has a heart attack." I said standing up and grabbing my tray. "Nice talking to you boys." I said walking off to my own table.

"Hey." I greeted Will as he plopped down in the seat next to mine.

"Hey." He said glancing over at Liam's table.

"Oh stop." I said hitting him on the arm.

"Sorry." He said grinning sheepishly. "So how was the first night?"

"Good, I slept fine. I think the better question is how was your first night without me?" I asked teasing him.

"I missed you." He said pulling me into him and hugging me."

"I missed you too." I confessed.

"Do we get to kill anybody yet?" John asked hopefully sitting down on my other side.

"No John. You do not get to commit murder and serve a life term in prison."

"Aw." He said looking crestfallen.

"Yes I know you were looking forward to your prison mate, especially at night."

"Hey! That's not funny."

"No of course not." I said making a serious face.

"I'm not gay!" He protested.

"Oh come on. I know a really nice guy I could hook you up with."

Shit! That did not just come out of my mouth!

"Really? Who would that be?" John asked raising an eyebrow.

"Um... Nobody you know. Some guy I knew back in the states." I covered, hoping he would drop it.

Thankfully he did. I had to be more careful about what I said. If I let Liam's secret slip, I was dead. The bell rang and we all headed off to our first period classes.

After first period I could tell today was going to be an awesome day. I got an A on my Literature paper, I had gotten a B on a pop quiz in Math, let me tell you that's a miracle in itself! The torture that I like to call basketball finally ended in P.E and we moved onto soccer. Oops. I mean football, at least that's what everyone else called it, not my best sport, but nothing was as bad as basketball. Lunch had been normal and now I was heading off to History with Liam. Yes, today was going to be an awesome day.

My day got even better when we walked into the classroom to find a substitute teacher sitting behind the desk, with a book in his hand and the words FREE DAY, written on the board behind his head.

I sat in my usual seat next to Liam. However, soon desk were clumped together in little groups around the room, various groups talking. Quinton, Hunter and three other boys that had a staring problem joined Liam and I.

"So Lily." Quinton said throwing an arm over the back of my chair.

"Quinton." I shot back looking from his arm to him.

"I was thinking, do you want to go out some time?"

Did this boy ever stop?

"I'm dating Will, you know that." I said shooting him a look.

"So what?" Hunter threw in.

"So that means, I'm in a relationship, which means I don't date other guys. That's called cheating." I said, trying to get it through his head.

"Like no one else has ever cheated."

"I'm not a cheater." I shot back.

"There's a first time for everything, or you could just dump him now and go out with me instead." He said smiling casually.

"No." I responded bluntly.

"I don't know what you see in him. I'm obliviously the better choice." Quinton said with a cheeky grin.

I took a deep breath and held it before letting it out slowly. There were so many things that I wanted to say, but the last thing I wanted was drama with my roommates. So instead of voicing all the reasons, that Will was better than Quinton aloud, I decided to ignore him and say them to myself in my head.

"I'm better looking."

'Will is model worthy.'

"I'm smarter."

'Will's a math genius!'

"I have more money."

'Money doesn't matter.'

"Are you even listening to me Lily?" Quinton asked waving a hand in front of my face.

The bell rang and I jumped out of my seat, heading for the door.

"God, she's got a nice ass." I heard Quinton remark as I left the room.

'Will has class.'

That night I crawled into my bed, and closed my eyes, hoping that I would get to experience the same dream from the night before. However, I've never been someone who has good luck.

I was standing looking down at the cold, marble tombstone of my parents. There wasn't another person around; there wasn't anything around. Just me and my parent's lifeless bodies buried six feet under my feet

"You should have been with them."

I turned around looking for where the voice had come from. All, I saw was empty space.

"You should have been in the car with them."

I snapped my head in the other direction trying to catch a glimpse of the mysterious person that the voice belonged to.

"Stop hiding the truth. Everyone will find out eventually, and when they do, they're going to leave, because you're a liar. You've hid secrets from them."

"SHUT UP!" I yelled into the empty air.

"So may lies."

"STOP!" I cried again trying to block out the voice.

"So many secrets."

I covered my ears, and squeezed my eyes shut. I could hear screaming. My eyes shot open, and I was no longer standing in front of my parent's grave. Everything was covered in darkness.

"Tell them."

"NO!"

I sat up in my bed, breathing heavily. I looked around the room and made sure I hadn't woken any of the boys up. They were all still asleep, quiet snore emitting from Quinton and Hunter.

I threw my covers aside and climbed out of my bed. I quietly made my way over to the closet and grabbed a pair of shoes and slipped them on. I slowly slipped out of the dorm and down the hallway. I jogged down the stair not wanting anyone to hear the elevator and wake up.

Walking out of the dorm, I wrapped my arms around my bare arms, wishing I had thought to bring a jacket. Stopping in the middle of the quad, I sat down on one of the wooden benches and pulled my knees to my chest.

"Lily?"

I quickly jerked my head around and saw Liam standing a short distance away.

"Liam. What are you doing out here?"

"I could ask you the same thing." He said sitting down next to me and smiling.

"I'm sorry. Did I wake you up?"

"Nah. I was already awake, couldn't sleep. You?"

"Uhh. Yeah, couldn't sleep." I lied.

"So many lies." The voice echoed in my head.

"Is something wrong? I get the feeling that something is bothering you." Liam said looking straight at me.

"No, I'm fine."

"So many lies."

"Lily?"

"Seriously, I'm fine. I just couldn't sleep and decided to come out here."

"And freeze to death?"

"I forgot my jacket."

"Lily, you're not telling me something."

"So many secrets."

I looked away from his piercing stare, trying to hide any emotion on my face.

"Lily, you can trust me." He said placing his hands on my shoulders and turning me back around.

Could I really trust him? What if he told everyone? What if he told Will?

"Liam, I-"

"I promise, whatever you say, you're secret is safe with me. You kept my secret and I'll keep yours. Trust me, it feels a lot better after you've told another person." He said with a grateful smile.

Maybe he was right, maybe it would be easier to deal with if one person knew. Just one.

"Okay, I'll tell you."

15

How do you tell someone your deepest, darkest secret? How do you confess that you haven't been completely honest with them, and that there is a whole other part to you that they never would have guessed existed? To tell them everything, to let them in and see you for what you really are.

This was the dilemma I was met with as I sat facing Liam, trying to decide how to tell him my secret. He didn't pressure me to talk, waiting silently, patiently, for me to talk to him when I was ready.

The silence surrounded us as I fought back and forth with myself, rather or not to tell him. Should I just get it all out in the open and go on like nothing had ever happened? There was no way that could happen. The minute I tell him everything would change. Liam wouldn't see me as carefree, hyper, bubbly Lily anymore. He would see me as poor, depressed, parentless Lily.

Could I get away with telling him another lie? Did I want to tell him another lie? No. It was time I stopped lying, I needed to tell someone. Someone needed to know, and right now, that someone was Liam. I took a deep breath in, ready to let my secret be known.

"My parents aren't coming to parents' day tomorrow." I said looking up at him.

"I know. You already told me they couldn't make it. It's okay, mine aren't coming either, remember? We can spend the day together; parentless. We can talk and gossip and eat junk until our heart's content. " He said looking at me with a smile.

I fought back tears, as I continued on. I wish it were as simple as that.

"I never told you why they couldn't make it."

Liam looked confused.

"My parents aren't coming because..."

I could feel the tears stinging the backs of my eyes, and my throat getting tighter.

"They're dead." It came out as a whisper as the long awaited tears slowly began to spill down my face.

Liam's arms wound around me, pulling me into him, my head automatically went to his chest as the sobs began to rack my body.

It felt like I was being shredded apart on the inside. Long, sharp, nails tearing at me, trying to destroy what was left of me. Telling Liam had made it all too real. When I had it locked up inside of me; it was almost as if they weren't dead. I thought that if I didn't tell anyone, if I didn't have to say it out loud, than it wasn't true, that my parents weren't dead. The harsh reality was they were, and that reality was finally settling in.

I brought my head up to look at Liam, tears still running down my face. He looked down at me, his eyes shinning. The way he looked at me had been one of the things I had feared most. I could see the pity in his eyes. I didn't want pity, I didn't want people to feel sorry for me, I didn't want people to treat me differently, but most of all, I didn't want my parents to be dead.

"I'm so sorry Lily."

I simply nodded my head, saying nothing.

"Is that why you're here?"

Another nod of my head, I didn't trust my voice.

His arms tightened around me and he leant his head on top of mine.

"You don't have to talk about it if you don't want to."

"No. It's time I did." I said sitting up.

He nodded his head, signaling me to begin when I was ready.

"It wasn't too long ago. Just before I came here. They went out for dinner one night and I told them I didn't want to go. The next thing I know, there are two police officers at my door." I wiped away new forming tears and continued on. "They told me that my parents had been hit by a drunk driver; they died on the scene. I should have been with them."

"Don't say that Lily!" Liam cried.

"I should have been with them, I should have died with them." I continued on, ignoring him.

Liam gripped my shoulders and shook me gently.

"Lily. You weren't meant to be with them that night. If you had gone you wouldn't be here."

"DON'T YOU GET IT!" I yelled at him breaking the still, quiet night around us. "THEY'RE DEAD. GONE. NEVER COMING BACK! I SHOULD HAVE BEEN WITH THEM! IT'S ALL MY FAULT!" I screamed at him, unleashing all of the emotions that I had kept bottled up inside of me.

He pulled me into his chest, refusing to release me through my protests. I began to quiet down and my tears slowed as he gently rubbed my back.

"It's not your fault. There is nothing you could have done. If you had been with them you wouldn't be here, and you're here for a reason. You weren't meant to be with them that night." He said quietly stroking my hair.

"But what if I could have done something? What if I had decided to go and taken time to get ready, then they wouldn't have left the restaurant when they did? What if I had told them to stay home? What if-"

"You can't live the rest of your life wondering what if." Liam cut in.

"I know, but-"

"No. You have to accept the fact that you couldn't have done anything to prevent it."

"I just miss them so much." I whispered, fresh tears falling down my face.

"It's okay. You have the right to cry, to mourn. It's okay to miss them."

I laid my head back against Liam's chest, and concentrated on matching my breathing with his slow, steady, heartbeats. In, thump, out, thump, in, thump, out, thump. I closed my eyes, feeling emotionally exhausted.

"Are you ready to go back up to the room?" His low voice rumbled, his chest lightly vibrating.

"Yeah."

We walked back up to our dorm in silence. Neither Quinton nor Hunter so much as stirred as we entered the room. I climbed into my bed next to Liam's and burrowed under the covers.

"Get some sleep Lily and don't worry about tomorrow. I'll be right there with you." Liam said trying to ease my fears.

I closed my eyes, trying not to think about parents' day, being only mere hours away. I prayed for a dreamless sleep, not wanting to encounter any more nightmares. One was enough for one night, or so I thought.

I stood once again in front of my parent's gravestone. The same emptiness surrounding me, almost suffocating me.

"Tell him." The familiar voice hissed.

I looked out into the endless space searching again for the voice I knew but couldn't place.

"I already told him." I retorted back at nothing.

"Tell him."

"I told him."

"Tell him."

I whipped around thinking I the voice had come from behind me. Instead I found myself face to face with Will.

"Tell him." The voice whispered, before fading away.

"Will I-"

"I don't want to hear it Lily."

"What?"

"I don't want to hear anymore of your lies."

"But Will-"

"Save it. I'm leaving." He said turning away from me and walking into the empty abyss.

"WILL!" I screamed chasing after his retreating figure.

No matter how fast I ran I couldn't reach him. Soon I could no longer see him. He was gone. Gone like my parents. Gone forever.

"Lily wake up."

My eyes snapped open returning me to the real world. Liam was standing over me shaking me gently.

"You okay?"

"Yeah, I'm fine." I said sitting up and swinging my feet over the side of my bed and placing them on the floor.

I stood up and headed towards the closet preparing to get ready for another day of classes, but then reality smacked me in the face. Today was parent's day, and my parents wouldn't be here. How was I going to avoid all of the questions? I would just have to avoid the boys at all cost. I could spend the day with Liam.

"You better get dressed Lily. You're late, Quinton and Hunter have already left." Liam called.

"Why? I'm not planning on leaving the room today."

"There is always an assembly to begin parents' day."

"Well, we don't have to go. Our parents aren't here."

"It's mandatory for all students."

"Oh come on! I don't think they'll notice two people missing." I said trying to convince him to stay locked away with me.

"I could get away with it, but seeing as you're the only girl. I'm pretty sure that would be obvious, and I think Will would notice the absence of his girlfriend."

I crossed my arms and pouted stomping into the closet to wear.

"Do we have to wear our uniforms?" I called from inside the closet.

"No. Just dress nicely."

Nicely. What was that supposed to mean? Did it mean no jeans? Maybe a sundress, or a skirt? No it was too cold for a dress, however a skirt could work. I pulled on a black skirt that fell just below my knees, and chose a gray and black cardigan, with pair of plain black pumps.

"How come I've never seen you wear this before?" Liam asked as I walked out of the closet and ran a brush through my hair.

"Maybe because we have to wear uniforms and other than that I only wear my pajamas."

"Good point. You look really pretty."

"Thanks. You look good too." I said as I looked at Liam. He was wearing a pair of black dress pants, with a dark green sweater.

"I only wish I had the legs to pull of the skirt you wearing." He said with a crooked smile.

"I wish I had your height so I wouldn't have to wear these heels."

I mirrored his smile.

"You ready?"

I took a deep breath in.

"I don't think I'll ever to be ready, but I guess I have to go out there."

He held open the door for me as I stepped out into the empty hallway. Everyone else must have already gone down to be with their parents at the assembly.

"Liam?"

"Hm?"

"About last night. No one else knows. So I would appreciate it if you didn't tell anyone." I said turning to look at him as we got into the elevator.

"You're secret is safe with me."

"As is yours." I said smiling as the doors slid closed.

We made our way across campus towards the large auditorium. I could faintly hear a low murmur of voice coming from inside. I stopped staring at the door, Liam at my side.

"You okay?"

"Yeah." I said taking a deep breath in and opening the door.

16

Every eye in the room fell on me. It was almost as if Liam wasn't even by my side. The parents stood next to their sons, looking at me, clearly I didn't belong. Then the whispers began to rise into the air. Their eyes looking down on me, judging me.

Well at least that's how I thought it was going to happen in my mind. To my surprise it was the complete and total opposite.

Liam and I stepped into the large building. There was no deafening silence, no accusatory looks, no snide remarks, no whispers; it was like I wasn't even there. I stumbled forward a bit as Liam gave me a gentle shove in the direction of a few vacant, metal, folding chairs, in the back of the auditorium.

I noticed that everyone else had started to find empty seats. I sat down in mine next to Liam. We were in the last row, nearest to the exit. Good for a quick escape. The noise increased as people began to file into the aisles bumping against the metal chairs.

My eyes scanned over the crowd looking for any of the boys' familiar faces. I spotted the twins right away. They were leading their parents down an empty row of seats. I smiled seeing how much they looked like their father.

Obviously they had gotten their hair and height from him. Their mother was a short, stout woman with light brown almost blonde hair.

Next I spotted Ian sitting down in between his mom and dad. He towered over both of them by a good six or seven inches, leading me to wonder where he had gotten his height.

Cal seemed to be trying to swat his mother's hand away as she licked her finger and rubbed it on his cheek, trying to remove what was probably left over breakfast. I let out a small laugh, remembering the lunch incident. I guess I was a bit like his mother. Liam cast me a sideways glance; I just smiled and kept my gaze forward.

I couldn't see any of the other boys. They seemed to be out of my range of sight. A deep voice rang out through the hall silencing any conversation that had been going on. I looked up towards the front of the hall seeing all of the teachers sitting in a line atop of a raised platform and a tall man speaking into the microphone. I spotted my uncle sitting closest to the man speaking.

"I would like to welcome all of the parents that are here today!"

"Who's that?" I whispered to Liam.

"That's just Mr. Owen. He pretty much runs the school."

"Then how come I've never seen him?"

"He doesn't exactly live here. He just comes in from time to time to make sure everything is running smoothly. Your uncle is basically the on campus head honcho, and he's the off campus head honcho."

"Oh." I said returning my gaze to the platform.

I tuned out his entire speech, about who knows what. I kept myself entertained by poking Liam in the side. He didn't seem interested in the speech either and started to poke me as well. I squirmed around in my chair trying to avoid his hand. He caught me off guard and poked me in the side.

I let out a small high-pitched squeak, before slapping a hand over my mouth and glaring at Liam. He put on an innocent face and acted as though he was being accused of something he didn't do.

We hadn't notice that this speech had ended and everyone was beginning to stand up and file out of the aisles. I stood up and brushed my hands down the back of my skirt smoothing out any wrinkles that had been there.

I glanced up and saw Will. He was heading towards the door with his parents. His dad was a tall man with chocolate colored hair like Will's and he seemed to be smiling at something Will had said. His mother on the other hand was short, with coal black hair, which she had pulled back into a twist at the nape of her neck.

I spun around on my heel and grabbed Liam's arm, dragging him out of the auditorium. I needed to get away from here as fast as possible. I needed to avoid Will and his parents.

"What's the rush?" Liam asked as I continued to drag him across the campus. "Besides, you're heading in the wrong direction. They always have a big get together in the cafeteria." He said easily pulling me back in the opposite direction.

"Liam no."

"Why?" He asked stopping in the middle of the walkway.

"Will and his parents." I said thinking that would explain everything.

"You get to meet his parents! Now I know the first time is always the hardest and a little bit awkward."

"Liam."

"You'll be okay though. I mean who wouldn't want you to date their son."
He rambled on dragging me closer and closer to the thing I wanted to be
farthest away from.

"No that's not it."

"You're just so adorable! They'll love you!"

I dug my heels into the ground and gave a sharp tug on his arm. He spun
around and looked at me confused.

"What?"

"I don't want to meet his parents. In fact I'm trying to avoid Will and them
at all costs. Parents are the last thing I want to see right now."

"Oh. Sorry."

"It's okay." I said smiling at him. "Now I do believe you promised that we
could pig out and gossip all day."

Liam's face lit up at the mention of gossip.

"You're right. I did, and I never break a promise. Especially if gossip is
involved."

We turned around and started back in the direction of our dorm.

"Lily!" A voice called from behind me.

I knew that voice anywhere.

I turned around and tried to avoid wincing when I saw Will walking
towards Liam and I.

"Hey." I smiled weakly.

"Come on. I want you to meet my parents." He said grabbing my hand and pulling me away from Liam.

I looked back and Liam gave me an apologetic smile, before turning around and walking away. Traitor.

I dutifully allowed Will to pull me through the throng of people, weaving in and out between bodies, as he made his way towards his parents. We came to a stop in front of the couple, Will stood there with a smile on his face his hand wrapped firmly around mine.

"Mum. Dad. I want you to meet my girlfriend, Lily."

"It's nice to meet you." Will's mom said with a large smile. "I'm Fiona."

"It's nice to meet you too." I said stretching out my hand in a greeting.

Instead I was engulfed in a tight embrace.

"Don't be silly dear! There's no need for stiff handshakes!" She said laughing, as she pulled back.

I was stunned and stood in silence.

"I'm Greg."

I turned my head to come face-to-chest, with Will's father.

"Hi." I squeaked out.

He let out a low chuckle that sounded close to Will's own laugh and smiled down at me.

"William has told us so much about you!"

I had to suppress a giggle as I noted the color rise in Will's cheeks at the use of his full name.

"He has?"

"Oh, yes! Of course we were quite surprised to learn that his girlfriend actually attended the same school, but he explained to us that your Uncle works here."

I felt a pang of guilt in my stomach; my lies were spreading.

"Where are your parents dear?" Fiona asked her bright smile still intact on her face.

The inevitable question.

"Oh. They couldn't make it." Yet another lie.

Well technically it wasn't a lie. They really couldn't make it, unless they happened to come back to life and claw their ways out of the ground. I just wasn't telling them why they couldn't make it.

"Why not?" Will asked, turning towards me looking confused at this new information.

"They had an extremely important business meeting." Okay now that was a lie. My parents had never even been business people.

Lying seemed to come to me as a second nature now.

"Oh."

"We were just heading down for lunch. Would you care to join us?" Greg asked.

"Sorry, but I have a previous engagement."

I turned towards Will and gave him a small smile. He placed a quick kiss on my cheek, which soon after was bright red. I took off in the opposite direction, glancing back over my shoulder to see Will doing the same, with a confused expression on his face. I could still hear his mom as she walked beside him.

"Such a nice girl." She said looking at her husband.

I hurried up to my dorm room, dashing inside and closing the door behind me. Safe. I walked in and saw Liam lounging on his bed with his hands behind his head. His eyes were closed; he was taking a nap.

I quietly crept over to my bed and grabbed my pillow. I raised it above my head and was ready to give him a good whack, when his right eye cracked open.

"I see someone's mad."

"You left me!"

"I couldn't very well tag along."

"Yeah, but-"

"You know I'm right." He said sitting up with a lazy smile.

"Doesn't mean I have to acknowledge it."

"So how were his parents?" He asked changing the subject.

"They're really nice. His mom seems really... friendly."

"I told you they would love you."

"Who doesn't love me?" I said flopping down next to him on the bed.

"Good point."

"Liam?"

"Yeah?"

"You never told me why your parents couldn't come."

"It's not important." He said his voice stiff.

"You okay?"

"Fine."

"I know that fine never means fine, you of all people should know that." I said turning towards him and crossing my legs under me.

"I don't want to talk about it." He retorted getting up and walking across the room and heading for the door.

"Where are you going?"

"For a walk."

I started to climb off of the bed to go with him, when he stopped me.

"By myself." He quickly walked out of the room and shut the door behind him with a little more force than necessary.

My body sagged back down onto the bed. Something was wrong. If something caused Liam to react like this it definitely wasn't good. No matter what he said he needed someone to talk to. He had proved to me that letting things out made you feel better.

Determined to go after him, I threw open the door and stepped out. I quickly backed into the room and shut the door swiftly. Will was heading down the hall, no doubt he had seen me.

Seconds later a soft knock rapped against the wooden door. I could feel myself stiffen. Maybe if I didn't move, didn't make a sound he would think he imagined seeing me and go away.

"Lily?"

Shit. He was not going to give up.

"Lily?"

I gave in and slowly opened the door to peak out.

"Hi!" I said with fake enthusiasm.

"Hey. Can I come in?"

"Yeah sure." I replied opening the door and letting him inside.

"I think we need to talk." He said walking over and sitting down on my bed, motioning for me to join him.

Oh God. Not this. I couldn't handle this right now. Those were the all time famous words. I knew what he was going to say next. 'It's not you, It's me.' I did not want to hear those words. I couldn't deal with hearing those words. I couldn't lose Will.

I slowly made my way over to my bed prolonging the inevitable.

"Lily, are you okay?"

"Yeah, I'm fine." I lied. "What did you want to talk about?"

"Well this morning you seemed to be acting kind of weird."

Was that what this was about? Hallelujah!

"Oh sorry. I guess I was a little tired." I said giving him a sheepish grin.

"Are you sure?"

"Yeah. Don't worry. I promise to get extra sleep tonight, so I'll be super bubbily tomorrow!"

"That's good to know." He said wrapping his arms around me.

I snuggled into his chest and smiled.

I could feel his warm lips on my jaw line, slowly making there way towards my lips. His lips captured mine in a soft embrace. I responded, moving my lips against his, lightly sucking on his lower lip. I could hear a low moan rumbling in his throat. His tongue gently moved against mine.

My hand tangled in his dark brown hair. His hand placed on the small of my back holding me in place. The other tracing slow circles on my arm. I pulled him in closer never wanting to let him go. He tasted so sweet; it was a mixture of honey and sugar.

Against my protests he pulled back and smiled.

"Do you know how lucky I am?" He said, my eyes still on his swollen lips.

"Yeah. Do you know how lucky I am?"

"Of course." He leant down and placed a kiss on my forehead.

He stood up grabbing my hand, pulling me towards the door.

"Where are we going?"

"I promised my parents we would meet up with them. They want to take us out to dinner."

The knot in my stomach tightened as we climbed down the stairs and out into the sunlight. My grip tightened around Will's hand as we walked.

"You okay?" He asked looking down at me as we continued to walk.

"Yeah, I'm fine."

But as we all know fine never means fine.

$$17$$

I sat in the back of Will's parents car as they drove us into town. I could feel my stomach doing flips as though it was trying out for the Olympics, my brain was already formulating different lies I could tell them to avoid any questions about my parents, and my skin was searing where Will had his hand placed on my knee, obviously picking up on my nervousness.

I looked at him out of the corner of my eye and caught him looking at me. I gave him a weak smile and fixed my gaze back on the passing scenery. A blur of green was all I could see as the car sped along past the trees.

After what seemed like endless hours of awkward silence the car pulled into a parking lot of a small restaurant. Will, being the gentleman he is, quickly clambered out of the car and rushed around to my side and held the door open for me.

I stepped out and met his cheeky smile.

"Thanks Will." I said to him as he closed the door.

"No problem." He responded shrugging his shoulders and grasping my hand with his, intertwining our fingers.

We followed Will's parents into the small restaurant and were immediately sat at a table in the corner of the restaurant.

"This is a nice place." I said as I glanced down at the menu.

"Oh, it's one of our favorites, we always come here on parent's day." Fiona chirped from across the table, her bright smile flashing across her face.

I noticed that Will had her smile. One side of her lip was just a bit higher than the other giving her and her son identical lopsided smiles.

I focused my concentration back onto the menu trying to decide what to order.

"So Lily why don't you tell us about yourself. We've heard William's version, I'm interested in hearing yours." Fiona smiled placing her menu down on the table.

"Well there's really not much to me. I grew up in Kentucky, I'm an only child, and I'm just a average girl."

"Oh I'm sure you're above and beyond average! Do you have any hobbies dear?"

"Well I used to play tennis, volleyball, and softball, but since moving here, I haven't really found the time or place to play."

"Tennis really?" Will's dad asked his eyebrows raised.

"Yea, I played for my old high school."

"I happen to play the game a bit myself." He said with a smile.

"Oh don't get him started, he's addicted to the sport." Fiona said rolling her eyes and throwing one of her beaming smiles at her husband.

"Yea dad's a bit of a tennis buff." Will chimed in.

"Don't listen to these two, they just don't appreciate the game."

I gave a short laugh before the waiter arrived at our table to take our orders.

After we had all placed our orders I excused myself to the restroom.

I pushed the door to the bathroom open and hurried in, my heels lightly clicking against the marble floor. I turned the cold water knob and placed my hands under the steady stream of water and brought them back up to my face.

I just needed to calm down, there was no need to worry, no need to panic. Even if they did bring up my parents I could just feed them one of my lies I had concocted on the drive here.

I took a few deep breathes, concentrating on keeping myself calm and collected, ran my fingers through my hair, pulled the hem of my shirt down a bit, plastered on a quick smile, and marched out of the restroom ready for battle.

"Are you okay?" Will whispered to me the second I sat down.

I threw a quick glance in his parents direction, they were quietly talking to each other as they ate their food that had came while I was gone.

"I'm fine. Why?" I whispered back as I picked up my fork and knife and began to eat my dinner.

"Nothing." He replied continuing to eat his dinner.

"I really do wish your parents could have been able to make it for parent's day Lily. We would love to meet them one day." Fiona stated.

I choked on the bit of steak that I had just put into my mouth. Will hit me on the back trying to help me swallow, but it being Will it wasn't exactly the lightest of taps and I just ended up coughing even more.

After I had finally stopped dieing, I cleared my throat and looked straight at Will's mom.

"I know they wanted to be here but they just couldn't find time to fit it in. It's no big deal really, I'm sure you'll meet them one day."

Everyone would meet them one day, they just had to die to do it.

"I still can't believe they didn't come. You're their daughter, they should have made time." Will said crossly next to me.

"William." His father scolded him.

"Sorry."

"No, it's okay Will. Seriously, I understand why they couldn't make it."

The conversation about my parents ended then and there. The rest of dinner consisted of various topics that were safe enough to talk about that I didn't have to lie anymore than I already had.

After we had all finished our meals and Will's parents had paid the check we all piled back into the car and headed back in the direction of the school. It was getting late and the sun had already set. Will's parents tried as best as they could to make small talk with me, but my short answers didn't help very much. I was exhausted and the last thing I wanted was to be bombarded with more questions.

The car came to a stop at the top of the drive leading to the quad and Will and I crawled out. Taking my hand we made our way around to the driver's side of the car to say goodbye to his parents.

"Take good care of her Will." His dad said smiling.

"And Lily make sure you keep him in line!" Fiona chimed in leaning across her seat so as to be seen.

"I will." We both replied at the same time with a small laugh.

"Oh and do tell your parents we said hello!" Fiona called as the car drove off.

My smile faltered for only a split second as Will and I waved and watched the car turn out onto the road and drive away from the school.

We made our way back to the dorms and into the front lobby. Just looking at the soft, overstuffed, couches made me want to curl up right there and sleep for the next two days. Unfortunately Will had other things on his mind.

He pulled me into his chest, his chin resting atop my head. Placing soft kisses down my temple and onto my cheek before reaching my lips and capturing them in a soft yet eager embrace. I could feel his hand on the small of my back beginning to slowly slide lower.

"Will." I pulled back from his kiss and met his disappointed gaze.

"What?"

"I'm tired." I said resting my head on his chest and closing my eyes.

"Okay okay." I could hear the smile in his voice.

We walked into the elevator and pressed the buttons for the second and third floor. Seconds later the doors opened with a soft ping and waited for me to step out. I gave Will one last kiss before stepping off of the elevator and into the hallway.

"Sweet dreams." He called with a smile as the doors slid shut and proceeded to take him up to his room.

I dragged myself, as best as I could in my heels, back to my room. Unlocking the door, I shuffled in and fell face down onto my bed.

"Someone's sleepy." I recognized Liam's voice coming from the bed next to me.

"Mhm." I grunted kicking my heels off and pulling the covers down.

"Aren't you going to change?"

"Mhm."

I pulled the covers up and curled into a ball, letting my head sink into the pillow and I started to drift off.

"Goodnight Lily." Liam chuckled and turned off the light.

Morning came far too soon, with the sun's rays peeking in through slanted blinds and resting right on my face. Groaning I flipped over and buried my face into my cool pillow.

Not five minutes later there was a knock on the door. I ignored the noise knowing one of the boys would get it and tried to go back to sleep. The knock came again, a bit louder this time.

"Liam answer the door." I mumbled into the pillow.

When I didn't get a response or hear feet shuffling towards the door, I lifted my head from the pillow and looked to Liam's bed, only to find it empty. I turned to look at Quinton's and Hunter's beds, but found them empty as well.

I groaned as a third, louder knock came from the door.

Dragging myself from my bed, I slowly made my way to the door and pried it open.

"Good morning sunshine!" Will greeted me.

"What time is it?" I asked leaning against the doorframe.

"Nine."

"It's Sunday Will."

"So?"

"That means I get to sleep in." I turned back around and headed for my bed, not bothering to close the door, and flopped back down, pulling my pillow to my chest.

"Oh come on Lily, you've got the rest of your life to sleep." Will complained coming into the room and sitting down on my bed.

"The rest of my life starts now then."

"Lily!" He whined like an impatient four year old.

"I'm tired Will."

"You were tired last night! Are those the same clothes?"

"Yea."

"You didn't change?"

"No."

"Well even though you look adorable you can't spend the day in the same clothes."

I could feel the bed lighten as Will stood up and went to do God knows what.

Minutes later, I was finally drifting back to sleep when I felt Will trying to tug my shirt off.

"Will!" I yelled as I sat up and pulled my shirt back down. "What the hell are you doing?"

"Seeing as you weren't going to, I decided to pick out your clothes and dress you."

"I am perfectly capable of dressing myself."

"Yea, but I thought it would be more fun if I did it." He said wiggling his eyebrows at me.

I let out a small laugh and playfully punched him in the arm. Only Will could make me laugh this early.

"So is that a yes Will you can dress me?"

"No. That's a Will you can turn around while I get dressed and no peeking."

"You're no fun." He pouted and turned around.

I looked at the end of my bed to see what clothes he had picked out and burst out laughing.

"What's so funny?" He asked still facing the other direction.

"You actually think I would wear this?"

"More of hoping you would."

"I think not."

I picked up the mini skirt and the super low cut shirt that was meant to be layered with another shirt, which Will had conviently forgotten, and walked back to the closet. I quickly pulled on a pair of jeans and a hoodie.

"You can turn around now."

Will jumped up and spun around.

"Well it's not exactly what I picked out, but you still look beautiful." He said walking over and placing a kiss on my cheek.

"Thanks." I said with a laugh. "You ready to go get some breakfast?" I asked walking towards the door.

Before I could reach the door, Will scooped me up in his arms and carried me back over to my bed. He put me down and crawled on top of me. His lips quickly made their way down my jaw line and to my biggest weakness my neck and my collar bone.

"Will." His name came out in an airy tone and he expertly nipped and licked at my neck.

"Yes?" He asked with a knowing tone. He knew this drove me wild.

"I thought we were going to go..." I trailed off not finishing my sentence as he began to lightly suck on my neck, spreading light kisses up and down the length of it.

His hands held my own above my head, keeping me from running my hands through his luscious locks of chocolate brown hair. His tongue tracing its way down to my collar bone, soon followed by little nips at the skin stretched across it.

"Oh God Will." I breathed out.

I closed my eyes and waited for more pleasure, when he suddenly stopped.

I opened my eyes to find his smiling face looking down at me.

"Come on Lily, we have to go get breakfast, can't lay around in bed all day." He said pulling me up.

"But Will!" I whined not caring about food any longer, only wanting his lips back on me.

"Nope, I think you've had enough for one morning." He said his lopsided grin spreading across his face as he took my hand and led me out the door and towards the cafeteria.

"So where have you two been?" Cal asked as Will and I sat down at the table.

I could feel the color rising in my face as I looked around the table at all of the knowing faces.

"We weren't doing anything any of you are thinking about right now." Will said looking around the table, a reassuring hand resting on top of mine.

"Sure you weren't." Jason said rolling his eyes.

I punched him in the arm and ignored his whines of how he was going to bruise and continued to eat my food, Will's fingers lazily playing with my own.

I looked up at him and caught his gaze, we gave each other a knowing smile.

"So what did you and your parents do yesterday Lily?" Oliver asked me.

I cringed on the inside before I answered.

"Oh, they couldn't make it."

"Why not?"

"They were busy." I answered dryly hoping Oliver would drop the subject.

"Well that's a lame ass excuse." John said deciding to join in on the conversation.

"It's not a big deal guys, they couldn't come, period, end of discussion." I said becoming annoyed.

They dropped the subject and returned to their food.

I picked up my fork and stabbed a piece of sausage, bringing it up to my mouth, I caught a glimpse of Liam out of the corner of my eye. It was obvious he had heard our discussion, his eyes were void of their usual sparkle, instead replaced with dull pity.

I immediately lost my appetite and put my fork back down. The same voice from my dream echoed in my ears.

"So many lies."

"I don't feel very good." I lied pushing away from the table and standing up.

"What's wrong?" Will asked standing as well.

"It's nothing just my stomach, I'm just going to go lay down for a bit."

"You want me to come with you?"

"No. I'll be fine, don't worry about it."

"Okay." Will said reluctantly before sitting back down.

I wound my way through the tables, heading towards the exit, as fast I could. Before I pushed through the doors that led outside I saw Liam getting up from his table and starting in my direction. A quick glance back at my table and I saw Will watching Liam making his way towards me, before Will got up and followed suit walking as fast as he could after Liam without making a scene.

I took off at a quick jog hoping I could make it back to my dorm room and fake being sick, before being confronted by either of the two.

I reached my dorm and fumbled around in my purse for the key.

"Lily." I heard Will's and Liam's voices yell out at the same time as the stepped off the elevator.

Without looking back I grabbed my key and jammed it into the lock. I pushed into the room and locked the door, praying that Liam had forgotten his key.

I scrambled under my covers, like a three year old hiding from the boogie man would, and pretended to be asleep, ignoring the knocks on the door.

I could hear Liam fumbling with his key to get the door open and silently cursed him for always remembering his key.

I flipped over onto my side, facing away from the door, as it opened and both boys stepped in and headed straight towards me.

18

I'm sure everyone has seen a horror movie where the poor victim is huddled in a corner or hiding under the bed or in the closet, cowering away from whatever horror has been chasing after said victim.

Well lets just say I was the victim in this particular horror flick and Will and Liam were the killers, monsters, whatever horror you could imagine.

I had the covers tightly pulled over my head and had reverted to curling up into the fetal position. My hood pulled over my head I tucked my head into my knees, just in case they pulled the covers off I could still be hidden, well not really, but it was worth a try.

"Lily." I heard Will's voice right next to my bed.

Somewhere in my mind I convinced myself if I had didn't make a sound, stopped breathing and just lay still, neither of them would be able to see me. I would be invisible and could just slip out the door unnoticed.

"Lily, stop acting like a three-year-old and come out from under the covers."

Will's tone tipped off that he was angry and annoyed.

"Lily, we just want to talk." Liam's soft, assuring voice chimed in.

"There's nothing for you and Lily to talk about. I'm just making sure she's feeling well. There's no need for you to even be here so you can just leave now." Will told Liam.

Oh boy, here we go.

"Well seeing as this is my room and Lily is my friend I have the right to be in here. You on the other hand did not have permission to come in, so you're lucky to even be in here right now." Liam snapped.

"Piss off Kalsen."

"Don't tell me to piss off! Get out of my room right now!" Liam retorted, no doubt a head bob thrown in.

Oh Liam please hold the gayness in. I silently pleaded under the covers listening to the two bicker back and forth. In my head I could clearly see Liam with his hand on his hip.

"This is Lily's room as much as it is yours and I think she wants me to stay! Don't you Lily?"

Damn. They hadn't forgotten that I was in the room. I stayed silent, trying to keep my last hope alive.

"She obviously doesn't." Liam spat triumph dripping from his voice.

"Lily?" Will asked his voice softer.

Shit. I hurt his feeling by not telling him I wanted him to stay. Damnit, a picture of a hurt Will, with his big puppy dog eyes and quivering bottom lip popped into my head and refused to leave.

"I want Will to stay." My voice came out weird, muffled by my clothes and the covers.

"See Lily wants me to stay! Now you can just see yourself out Kalsen."

"I want Liam to stay too." I protested from my cocoon of cloth.

"What?" Will asked puzzled.

I felt the warmth of the covers disappear as Will lifted my fortress off of me and left me curled in a tight ball, defenseless and vulnerable. I felt the mattress sink on both sides, Will on one side, Liam on the other. Now I was trapped, with one of them on each side there was no way I was getting out of this.

We sat there for awhile, no one saying a word, the awkward silence filling the room until it almost smothered me. Will finally broke the silence.

"What's gotten into you lately Lily?"

I uncurled and sat up to face him.

"What do you mean?" I asked scrunching my eyebrows together and feigning innocence.

"You've been acting really strange, you've been saying you don't feel well and then the next time I talk to you you're perfectly fine, and whenever I try to bring up the subject you just brush it off and put on a smile."

"I don't know what you're talking about." I replied looking away. Unfortunately the only place to look was towards Liam, whom sat arms crossed with a stern look on his face.

"I think you do know what he's talking about Lily." Liam said looking at me with his piercing gaze.

"I don't think you know what I'm talking about Kalsen, so you can just butt out." Will snapped before I could respond.

"Oh I know a lot more than you do!" Liam clasped his hand over his mouth the second the words came out.

"LIAM!" I yelled turning towards him.

"What's he talking about Lily?" Will asked looking hurt.

"I don't know." I said trying to cover it up.

"I think you should tell him." Liam said standing up from the bed and heading towards the door.

I jumped up from my spot on the bed and charged after him. How could he do that? I had never pressured him to share his secret. I had respected him enough to keep quiet, and here he was, in front of Will, telling me to confess my secret. The nerve!

"Liam Kalsen!" I screamed grabbing his shoulder and turning him around. "How dare you try to tell me to do that! I NEVER pressured you in any way to tell-" My words were cut short by Will.

"So you're cheating on me with him." He said it as though it was a proven fact not a question.

"What? No!" I defended, turning around almost smacking into Will's chest.

"No, Lily. I get it, you can stop lying. I should have seen it earlier, it was so obvious that you and Liam had something going on, I just can't believe I was stupid enough to ask you to be my girlfriend."

I stood in silence, hot tears stinging the back of my eyes, as Will pushed past me.

"Will I'm-"

He cut me off again.

"Stop lying Lily." He grabbed the handle to the door and twisted it.

"She's not cheating on you." Liam said coming to my defense.

"And I'm supposed to believe you?" Will said rolling his eyes and opening the door.

Liam's hand came flying through the air, and slammed against the door, closing it and almost taking Will's nose off in the process.

"She's not cheating on you, especially not with me." He said beginning to glare at Will.

"Give me one good reason why I should believe the two of you."

"Because I'm gay."

"Liam!"

What had I done now? Of course I was mad at Liam for trying to oust my secret, but that didn't mean that both of our secrets had to be out. If I had only been honest with everyone from the start none of this would be happening. Will and I wouldn't be on the verge of a breakup, Liam wouldn't have to tell anyone he was gay, and I wouldn't have to lie everyday.

"No, Lily it's okay. It's my fault, I shouldn't have said what I did." He said shrugging his shoulders.

"Liam-"

"What?" Will asked once again cutting me off, the boy was really starting to make a habit out of that.

"I'm gay." Liam said putting a smile

"I don't understand." Will said looking between Liam and myself.

"I like boys, I prefer penis, I don't like boobs. Need I go into more detail because if you want I can tell you about the summer in Paris with this incredibly sexy French boy."

"No! I don't need any details." Will said holding up his hand, and closing his eyes, obviously trying to block out the mental image that was already forming in his brain.

"What I still don't understand though is what you wanted Lily to tell me. Did you want her to tell me you're gay?"

"No, Will that's not it." I said running my hands through my hair.

I guess this was it, there really was no way out of it this time. I couldn't just blow it off like the other times. We had basically said everything leading up to it and to pretend that nothing was wrong would just lead to bigger problems.

"Do you mind giving us some time to ourselves?" I asked looking at Liam.

"No problem, you two need some time to talk. If you need me just call my cell." Liam said opening the door. "Oh and Will."

"Yea?"

"Don't tell anyone what I told you, no one else, other than Lily, knows."

"I won't." Will said sitting down on the bed.

"Good because if you do, I'll tie you to a chair and tell you every single detail about my summer in Paris, and I do mean every detail. Bye!" Liam closed the door with a cheery smile.

I turned towards Will and could have sworn he was a shade lighter than usual. Liam was going to put this boy in his grave if he kept on threatening him with those things.

I walked over and sat down next to will and tucked my legs underneath myself.

"Will I need to tell you something." I said nervously playing with my fingers.

"You're not gay too, are you?" He asked looking nervously at me.

"No, I'm not gay." I reassured him with a small laugh.

"And you're not dating Liam?"

"Obviously not."

"Well I don't see what could be so awful then." Will said his mood seeming to lighten as a small smile popped onto his face.

I took in a deep breath preparing myself to come clean.

"I've been lying to you."

"Lying? What about?" His smile turning into a frown.

"My parents." I said focusing my gaze on the floor and the pattern I was tracing into the carpet with my toe.

"Your parents? Why would you lie about your parents?"

"It's complicated."

"Oh, God! Is general McKain your dad? I mean him being your uncle was terrifying enough but if he's your dad, I might have to go into the witness protection program one day!" Will hysterically rambled.

"No Will, he's just my uncle."

"Well that's a relief."

"If I tell you something can I trust you, that you won't tell anyone else, or treat me differently?" I asked finally looking up from the floor to meet Will's gaze.

"Of course you can Lily." He said his eyes softening. "I want you to be able to tell me everything, you can completely trust me.'

"Okay, I trust you Will."

I took in one last deep breath before plunging head first into my story.

"I told you that my parents couldn't make it to parents day because they were busy. Well they had another reason that they couldn't make it."

"There's no excuse for not coming to see their only daughter." Will said crossly.

"Yes there is." I said quietly, feeling the first tears form behind my eyes. "They're dead."

The tears slipped down my cheeks faster than I thought they would. They didn't come in great, heaving, sobs or bone rattling cries. They came silently one by one, gently falling down my face.

"Oh Lily."

"I can understand if you don't want to be with me anymore." I said looking away.

"What? Why wouldn't I want to be with you?" He asked gently pulling my face back to look at him.

"Because I'm a liar."

"Lily, I don't care if you lied about your parents. What I care about is you and why you felt the need to hide this from me." He murmured into my hair as he pulled me into his lap and wrapped his arms around me. "Why didn't you tell me, or anyone for that matter?"

"I told Liam." I meekly protested.

I could feel Will's chest expand and then return to normal as he took in a deep breath and let it out.

"I meant one of us." He said stressing the last word.

I knew what he meant when he said us. He was talking about the other boys, our circle of friends, minus Liam because technically he wasn't in our circle, he was in my circle.

"I was afraid." I said

"Of what?" He asked pulling back to look at me.

When Will pulled back I had my answer. His eyes were no longer the same deep chocolate brown eyes filled with happiness and spontaneity, instead they were a dull reflection of what they once were, the joy they had held had been suppressed and in its place shone forth sadness and pity. The way he looked at me, as if I was an injured animal that was going to have to be put down, I had never wanted for him to look at me with those eyes.

"That." I said looking away from him and focusing on the door.

"What?" He asked trying to make me look at him again, I refused and kept my gaze forward.

"The way you're looking at me. Like I'm the most pathetic thing you've ever seen." My voice had taken on a cold edge.

"Lily, I don't think of you like that and you know it." Will defended sternly.

"You're doing it right now!" I retorted whipping around in looking him in the eyes. "I can see the pity! I hate it!" I yelled at him and pushed away.

"Lily!" Will called after me.

"No Will. I need some time to think. I'll talk to you later." I said opening the door and stepping out.

I turned around to close the door, to see Will sitting on my bed looking defeated and hurt.

"I'm sorry." I said barely audible, before closing the door and taking off down the hallway.

I jammed my hands into the front pocket on my hoodie and took off across the quad. I reached the boundaries of the school grounds where the stone entrance sign was, proclaiming the name of the school.

I hadn't planned on leaving the school grounds, but right then I couldn't have cared less if I got in trouble or if I even got kicked out of the school. Even though it was Sunday and there were no classes, students still weren't allowed to leave school grounds, except for Saturdays.

With out another thought I started down the road towards the small town I had been to with the boys before. No one would know where I had gone and I would be back before anyone noticed and came looking for me.

Upon arriving in town, I strolled down the small sidewalk, past all of the shops, that normally would have enticed me inside. Instead, I opted for a small stone bench on the far side of a small park.

There was hardly anyone at the park for it being a Sunday, the cool weather must have kept people indoors.

I pulled my hood up over my head and my knees into my chest. I rested my chin on my knees and stared out into the trees.

As hard as I tried I couldn't forget the way Will had looked at me. Worse, what did he think of me now? Did he think I was an emotionally unstable psycho? Had he decided that it he would be better off with out me? Would he be better off without me? Would I be better off without Will?

I sat on the cold, stone bench, ignoring the numbness that now resided in my butt, and thought about all of the questions running through my head.

Was I an emotionally unstable psycho?

No, I was defiantly not a psycho. Emotionally unstable? No, I didn't think I was that either. I wasn't exactly sure what I was, other than a liar.

Would Will be better off without me?

I couldn't come up with an answer to that one, I didn't know what he was thinking or feeling and no matter how hard I thought I couldn't imagine what he must be thinking right now.

Would I be better off without Will?

This was the hardest question. Would I? Why had I even thought of that?

After hours of thinking I had only come up with more questions.

Some of my questions could only be answered by Will, some of my questions would never be answered, and some of my questions had answers that I didn't even want to think about the consequences.

19

- -

I couldn't begin to tell you how long I sat in that small park, my butt plastered to the cold stone bench; thoughts whirring around in my head so fast it made me dizzy. What I could tell you though was it was now dark. Dark was bad, dark meant that I had indeed spent a great deal of time in this park. Dark meant trouble.

Unfolding my legs from beneath me, I climbed off of the bench and stretched my arms up towards the sky dotted with tiny stars. My sleeves slid down and exposed my bare skin, sending goose bumps down my arms. I guess dark and cold went hand-in-hand.

I pulled my hoodie tighter around me and started back towards the school. All of the lights in the shop windows had already been turned off, leaving me to rely on memory to find my way back down the streets.

Something I had never been very good at was directions. Of course I knew left from right, but north, south, east, and west; not a clue. I took my best guess and headed off in what I thought would be the general direction of the school. All I really had to do was find the main road and I would be good.

Apparently I'm not very good at guessing either. This was definitely not the way back to school. I turned around and started back the way I had come.

Shit. Shit. Shit. None of this looked familiar! I didn't recognize any of the street names, or dark store windows. Where was I?

My breath started to quicken. I had always been easily scared, and I'll admit that I am still afraid of the dark. I blame my over active imagination, I would be fine if it weren't for the fact that whenever I was in the dark, my mind would immediately dig up all of the horror movies I had ever seen.

I had to think, find the main road, ask for directions, something.

Of course! Stupid me, I'll just call Liam, he did say if I needed anything to call his cell.

I reached into my pocket and pulled out my phone, quickly scanning through the list of names and hitting the send button on Liam's.

Ring. Ring. Ring.

"Damnit. Pick up Liam." I mumbled.

Ring. Ri-

"Hello?" Liam answered his voice sounding frantic.

"Hey Li-"

"Oh My God! Lily!"

"Uh, yea. Can you not scream?"

"Where the hell are you?" Liam continued to scream.

"I don't know. I went into the town and got lost. I'm on some street called-" I looked around and found a small street sign. "Pine Oak Street."

"SHE'S ON PINE OAK STREET!" I heard Liam scream away from the phone.

"Liam! Stop screaming, just tell me how to get back." I said getting irritated.

"No! Don't move, he's coming to get you."

"Who?" I asked puzzled.

"Your Uncle."

"Liam! No! Don't tell him I snuck out! He'll kill me!"

"Too late, he just took off in his car. The whole school has been looking for you."

"What? Why?"

"You disappeared, you've been gone since this morning. We thought you'd been kidnapped or eaten by a monster."

"Eaten by a monster?"

"Okay, so that was my theory, but who knows." I could almost see him rolling his eyes now.

"Liam, you're being stupid."

"I'm stupid? You're the one that ran off in a foreign country, not knowing where anything was, without telling anyone!"

"Well I-"

"No Lily!" Liam cut me off. "It was irresponsible and foolish. You could have gotten hurt or worse." He was getting hysterical.

"Liam. I'm fine. I just stayed out too late and got lost." I tried to calm him down a reassure him.

"Oh that's it?" His tone was sarcastic.

"Uh... yeah."

"Well did you ever once think of telling someone where you were going before you just up and left? Hm? Maybe a note on the door, or a text, or hell just leave a trail of breadcrumbs!"

Great. Now Liam was mad at me.

"Liam, calm down. I'm sorry, I'll tell someone next time, I promise."

"There isn't going to be a next time."

Oh shit.

That definitely wasn't Liam's voice.

Slowly I turned around ignoring Liam's voice coming through on the other end of the phone. My Uncle was standing outside of his jeep, he must have been going pretty damn fast to get here that soon.

His face was set into a hard scowl, his eyes almost black.

"Uh... I gotta go Liam." I said closing my phone, just as he began to protest.

"Get in the car." His voice was deep and grave.

Shit.

Keeping my eyes on the ground, because God knows if I had looked him in the eye, I would have been the newest stone statue in the park, I trudged over and lowered myself into the passenger seat.

Uncle Eric walked around and got into the driver's seat, slamming the door hard enough to shake the small jeep. Turning the key, the jeep rumbled back to life and he started back the way he had came, obviously at a much slower pace.

The silence was smothering me, choking out every last bit of air I had stored up in my lungs.

"I'm sorry." I said, finally breaking the silence.

He remained quiet his eyes straight ahead, however, I noticed that his grip on the steering wheel tightened. He took in a deep breath and held it for a considerably long time, before letting it back out.

I decided that it would be best if I kept my mouth shut for the rest of the ride.

It didn't take long for us to get back to the campus, and that just made me feel stupid. To know that I was a few minutes drive away. God I can't even be get myself lost decently.

"Lily!" Several voice blended together as a stampede of boys rushed towards me, Will leading the pack.

"Are you okay?" Will asked enveloping me into a hug, then turning me around looking for any signs of damage.

"I'm fine." I said quietly.

"Lily, follow me." Uncle Eric said.

Whether he was glaring at Will or I, I couldn't tell.

I looked back at the boys and shrugged my shoulders before turning and following my Uncle; my infinite doom.

Everything was quiet... until he closed the door. That's when the ticking time bomb exploded.

"What the hell were you thinking!" He yelled.

"I-"

"No! You weren't even thinking!"

"But-"

"No buts Lily. You ran off by yourself, you didn't tell anyone where you were going, you didn't even know where you were going!"

I winced as he yelled at me, his voice becoming louder with every word.

"I'm sorry." I said, trying anything to make him quit yelling.

"Sorry doesn't fix everything Lily."

"I'm sor-" I stopped myself before I could finish.

Uncle Eric walked around and slumped down in his chair behind the desk. Running his hands through his graying hair and over his face.

"Lily, I think it would be best if I made arrangements for you to attend another school." He said quietly looking up at me.

"What? No!" I cried, my eyes pleading, my mind frantic.

"Lily, it's obvious that this wasn't the best environment for you. I know a very nice boarding school in Switzerland." He said trying to reason with me.

"No! You can't do that."

"Lily-"

"NO!" I screamed.

I could feel the tears starting to slide down my face.

"I can't leave. This is what I need right now, I need something stable. If you take me away from here I don't know what I'm going to do. I have a boyfriend and friends and I like it here and I feel safe here and I need this and... and..." My voice broke off with the thought of having to leave this all behind.

"Lily-"

"Please just listen to me!" I pleaded. "I can't take leaving everything again. I can't have everything that means something to me ripped away, not again. I can't do it. This place is my home now and if I have to leave it would kill whatever is left inside of me."

The tears were pouring out of me at this point, I must have looked a mess because all I could see in my uncle's eyes was pity.

I wish people would stop looking at me like that.

It was silent for a long time, besides the small sniffles that I was making.

"Okay." Uncle Eric finally said.

"What?" I asked, wiping my nose with my sleeve.

"You can stay." He said with a sigh.

"Seriously?" I asked jumping up from my chair.

"Yes."

"Oh my God! Thank you! Thank you! Thank you!" Running over behind the desk, I wrapped my arms around him and squeezed as tight as I could.

"But, if you pull anything like what you did today ever again, there will be no second chances. You will be on a plane to Switzerland the very next day."

"I won't." I promised as I continued to squeeze him. "You're the most fantabulous Uncle ever!" I squealed with one last hug, before running out the door to find Will.

"Fantabulous?" He said looking puzzled at his niece's retreating form.

I dashed across campus and right past the elevator in my dorm, opting for sprinting up the three flights of stairs and down the hall to Will's dorm.

I couldn't stop smiling as I pounded my fist into the door.

Without a second thought, I pounced on the person who opened the door.

"I get to stay!" I exclaimed looking down at who I expected to be Will.

"Well... that's lovely, but your crushing my chest, and I don't think Will would appreciate you straddling me." Oliver said looking up from under me.

"Oops. Sorry, Ollie." I said jumping up and helping him off the floor.

"Ollie?" Will said, walking into the room.

"Will!' I exclaimed as I tackled him.

Thankfully, we landed on the closest bed.

"I get to stay!" I said, moments later, my lips crashing down on his.

"I hate to break up this... wonderful moment... but where exactly were you going Lily?" Ian asked from the next bed.

Pulling away from Will, both of our faces a bit red, I sat up in Will's lap.

"Boarding school in Switzerland."

"What?" Will asked panicked.

"Don't worry, my Uncle gave me a second chance and I get to stay, as long as I don't screw up again."

"Well then I think the last thing you're Uncle really wants to see is you making out with Will." Ian said.

"We don't want to see that." Oliver said turning away.

"Fine. I better go anyways." I said climbing off of Will's lap. "See you tomorrow at breakfast." I called as I shut the door.

It was then that it hit me, I was extremely exhausted. All of this drama had worn me out and what I needed right now was a good night of sleep before classes started back up again tomorrow.

I dragged myself back to my dorm, the thoughts of my soft sheets and warm covers coaxing me forward.

I couldn't have taken a single step in the room before I found myself lying on my back in the hallway.

"You're okay!" Liam squealed, his arms wrapped around me.

"Well I was, but now I think I have a minor concussion." I retorted from under him.

"Stop being such a baby." He said as he hauled me to my feet and let me into the room.

"So, tell me what happened." Liam said flouncing across the room to and plopping onto his bed.

I looked around and noticed that both Quinton and Hunter were snoring quietly in their beds. How I envied them.

"Not now Liam, I'm exhausted." I groaned, falling face first into my pillow.

"But I'm not." He protested.

"Tomorrow."

"Tonight."

"If you don't let me go to sleep, I won't leave a trail of breadcrumbs next time, I'll leave locks of your hair, that I cut off in the night." I warned.

"No!" He squeaked grabbing his precious hair. "You win... this time, but I want all the details tomorrow."

I didn't even have to respond, I was already fading quickly into what would be a sleep without nightmare, something I hadn't had in a very, very long time.

20

For the last month, I've been very careful and aware of everything I've done. I made sure to do all my homework, get good test grades, and hell, I even restrained myself from jumping Will's gorgeous bones in front of everyone. After all, one more mistake and my ass was on a plain to Switzerland, and I'm pretty sure one of the things on my uncle's list that would put my ass on that plain was overly zealous public displays of affection.

Of course Will was not happy when I pushed him away in the empty hallways that my uncle might happen to be lurking in.

"Will." I sigh removing his hands from my hips.

"Ah, come on Lily. It's not like I'm going to jump you in the middle of the hall... even though that's a tempting idea." He said, his eyes roaming over my body shamelessly.

"So you would rather ravish me in a hallway once and then see my shipped off to Switzerland?" I said, eyeing him.

"No." He grumbled. "But I wouldn't mind the ravishing part." I heard him mumble under his breath.

"We've talked about that Will. I'm not ready." I said lecturing him once again.

"I know, I know." He said smiling, while caressing the side of my face.

"You better get to training; I don't want you to get in trouble again." I stated, thinking about last week when Will showed up late to training and had to stay an hour later.

"Yea, I don't want to relive and extra hour with your Uncle by myself. He's a very intimidating man you know, " he said.

"Yes, I know." I sighed remembering the threat that still hung in the air.

I headed off in the opposite direction of Will.

Upon opening my door, I found Liam sprawled across his bed with one arm covering his eyes.

"Liam?" I asked puzzled to why he wasn't at training.

He lazily picked his arm up and looked at me with bloodshot eyes.

"What's wrong?" I asked immediately worried that something was wrong.

"Nothing, I'm just stressed." He said sitting up and pressing the palms of his hands into his eyes.

"About what?" I asked flopping down on his bed next to him.

"Just stupid stuff." He mumbled.

"Well, it can't be that stupid if it's gotten you upset." I replied.

"I didn't say I was upset, just stressed." He stated defensively.

"Liam, your eyes are blood red as though you've been crying for awhile."

"So?" He asked.

"So, that means there has to be something wrong." I said looking at him.

"Nothing is wrong, everything is peachy keen!" He beamed at me, his smile wide and bright, but it wasn't his usual Liam smile.

"Well you know if you ever need to talk to me, I'm here. You were there for me and I'm fully ready to return the favor." I gave him a small smile.

"You should really work for Hallmark when you get older." He said shoving me gently.

"And you should work for Cosmopolitan." I shot back.

"Me?" He asked.

"Yeah you. You could write for the fashion column or you could give sex advice." I replied with a smile on my face.

"I'm not the one getting all touchy feely in the hallways!" My mouth dropped open. "Oh yes, I've seen you two getting cozy when you think no one is around." He said pointing a finger at me.

"Stalker!" I gasped out.

"It's not my fault I just happen to be walking down a hallway inhabited by two lovebirds." He said.

"Oh shut it, you're just jealous because you're not getting any." I retorted crossing my arms.

"YOU'VE HAD SEX!" Liam screeched, his eyes lighting up with excitement. "Details." He demanded crossing his legs.

"I haven't had sex!" I protested.

"You just said that I was jealous that I wasn't getting any, which is of course true, but that means that you're the lucky one getting some! Tell." He nagged.

"I swear Liam, I'm still a virgin. I didn't mean it like that." I told him.

"Hmph. Well you're no fun." He replied.

"Sorry, I'm not a whore like you." I teased.

"Oh, one, one-night stand in the Bahamas and I'm a whore?" He asked with an amused expression.

"What about the guy in Paris?" I asked him.

"He was a summer romance, that doesn't count." He shrugged it off.

"Irish hunk?" I asked, loving how I teased him with his affairs.

"We dated." He stated.

"Madrid model?"

"Oh, you would have done him too." He defended. "Anyways, enough about my escapades. What about yours?" Liam asked turning towards me.

"I don't have an escapades; virgin remember." I said forming a V with my fingers.

"Just because you're a virgin doesn't mean you can't have any fun; there are plenty of other things you could have done." He said, wiggling his eyebrows.

"Well I mean we've done a few things, but nowhere near sex." I told him, starting to blush.

"So what have you done then?" He asked edging closer.

I knew my face was red, I could almost feel the heat coming off of me.

"Well, uh, I... we've-" I was at a loss for words.

The loud bang of the door and the sounds of Quinton's and Hunter's voices saved me. I never thought I would be so glad to see those two.

I gave Liam a sheepish smile and slipped off the bed.

"I'm going to see Will, I'll see you at dinner." I said as I wave him goodbye.

"Don't do anything I wouldn't do." Liam replied with an exaggerated wink.

Rolling my eyes, I walked out of the room and jogged up the stairs.

I caught Will right before he followed the other boys into his room.

"Hey." I smiled catching him around the waist.

"Hey." He twisted around in my grip and kissed me on the forehead.

"Miss me?" I asked, staring into his eyes. I'm a really lucky girl.

"Always." He replied, staring at me with pure love and adoration.

"Well go shower, I'll wait for you and we can go down to dinner together." I told him.

"Are you insinuating that I smell?" He acted offended.

"Yep, you stink. Now go get clean." I teased him.

"Admit it, you think I'm sexy when I sweat." He said pulling me closer to him by his hips.

My face reddened slightly.

"Get a room you two!" Oliver yelled from inside.

Will gave him the finger.

"Watch it Oliver or I'll make sure it's your bed!" I said poking my head around Will's frame.

"You two better not EVER touch my bed!" Oliver warned.

"Then learn to keep your mouth shut." I teased.

"Oh that reminds me." Will mumbled.

"Of what?" I asked.

"I'll tell you at dinner, because apparently I offend you with my manly stench." Will said before darting into his room to grab a change of clothes and a towel, before heading down the hall to the showers.

Walking into the room, I plopped down on Will's bed.

"So what are you doing for the holidays Lily?" He asked me.

Christmas was fast approaching and the weather had gotten bitterly cold around here. I was used to cold winter weather, but this was just an extreme I had never experienced. There had been chatter all week long about who was going where with whom, or what they were getting other people for gifts, or far off islands with warm weather that the lucky were setting off to.

I mostly tried to block out all of the boys excited conversation at their two weeks of freedom. I had heard that some boys were staying at school, so naturally I assumed that I would just stay behind and relax in my empty dorm.

"I'm staying here." I answered.

"What? Seriously? That sucks." Oliver said sympathetically.

Apparently Oliver and his family were jet setting off to Jamaica to spend time with his retired grandparents.

"It won't be too bad, I'll have to dorm to myself and it will finally be quiet around here." I lied.

Of course there was the fact that Will wouldn't be around. I didn't like the idea of spending two weeks without him, but who was I to stop him from having a good holiday?

"Better?" Will whispered.

I jumped hearing Will's deep voice so close to my ear. I could detect a faint smell of soap.

"Much better." I said turning around. Our lips met and I could feel the heat of his lips mold against mine.

"Stop it!" Oliver whined.

"We're not on your bed." I said pulling away from Will.

"But I can still see you." Oliver complained.

"Oliver, make sure you get laid over the holidays so you won't be so up-tight." I said standing up and dragging Will out the door before Oliver could retort.

"Now how come you tell Oliver to get laid, but not me." Will pouted in the elevator.

"Because, he can go out and have a one night stand, you're stuck with me." I stated.

"I think I got the better end of this." He said smirking at me.

The elevator dinged and we got off.

"Shit." I said wrapping my arms around myself.

I had forgotten to grab my coat on my way out and the cold wind whipped through my long sleeved shirt.

Both of us hurried through the quad and into the welcoming warmth of the cafeteria. Only a few people lingered around or sat at table seeing as we were earlier than usual.

After getting our food and sitting down at our presently abandoned table I turned to Will.

"So, what you want to tell me?" I enquired.

"Well it's more of something I wanted to ask you." He replied.

"Go on." I said propping my chin on my closed fist.

"I was wondering if you wanted to come home with me for the holidays. I already asked my parents and they were very excited about the idea of you coming." Will said smiling at me.

"You have no idea how great that would be!" I beamed throwing my arms around him.

"So I take that as a yes." He said, smiling from ear to ear.

"Yes... from me, but I still have to ask my uncle." I said, now worried that my uncle would deny me the chance to go with Will.

"I'm sure he'll say yes, you've been on your best behavior this past month." He assured me.

"I'll go talk to him after dinner." I said.

Wrapping my arms around me as tightly as I possibly could, I rushed across the campus to my uncle's office. I entered without knocking, not being able to stand the cold a minute longer.

"Hello Lily." My uncle said looking up from a few papers that lay scattered across his desk.

"Hey." I said sliding into the seat in front of his desk. "Um, I was wondering if it would be okay if I went with Will to his home for the holidays?" I asked getting directly to the point.

He seemed taken aback by my question. I held my breath and prayed that he wouldn't say no.

"You want my permission to spend two weeks at your boyfriend's home?" He asked as though he hadn't heard the question correctly.

"Um, yea." I replied. Hope he agrees.

"Well, your grades have improved and I haven't heard of you getting into any type of trouble or causing any problems lately, so I think that would be okay." He answered.

"Thank you so much." I said standing up and walking around his desk and giving him a hug.

"Just make sure you stay out of trouble." He remimded me.

"I will." I promised as I walked back out in the chilly cold, happy to deliver the news to Will.